Erle Stanley Gardner and The Murder Room

〉〉〉 This title is part of The Murder Room, our series dedicated to making available out-of-print or hard-to-find titles by classic crime writers.

Crime fiction has always held up a mirror to society. The Victorians were fascinated by sensational murder and the emerging science of detection; now we are obsessed with the forensic detail of violent death. And no other genre has so captivated and enthralled readers.

Vast troves of classic crime writing have for a long time been unavailable to all but the most dedicated frequenters of second-hand bookshops. The advent of digital publishing means that we are now able to bring you the backlists of a huge range of titles by classic and contemporary crime writers, some of which have been out of print for decades.

From the genteel amateur private eyes of the Golden Age and the femmes fatales of pulp fiction, to the morally ambiguous hard-boiled detectives of mid twentieth-century America and their descendants who walk our twenty-first century streets, The Murder Room has it all. 〉〉〉

The Murder Room
Where Criminal Minds Meet

themurderroom.com

T0345410

Erle Stanley Gardner (1889–1970)

Born in Malden, Massachusetts, Erle Stanley Gardner left school in 1909 and attended Valparaiso University School of Law in Indiana for just one month before he was suspended for focusing more on his hobby of boxing that his academic studies. Soon after, he settled in California, where he taught himself the law and passed the state bar exam in 1911. The practise of law never held much interest for him, however, apart from as it pertained to trial strategy, and in his spare time he began to write for the pulp magazines that gave Dashiell Hammett and Raymond Chandler their start. Not long after the publication of his first novel, *The Case of the Velvet Claws*, featuring Perry Mason, he gave up his legal practice to write full time. He had one daughter, Grace, with his first wife, Natalie, from whom he later separated. In 1968 Gardner married his long-term secretary, Agnes Jean Bethell, whom he professed to be the real 'Della Street', Perry Mason's sole (although unacknowledged) love interest. He was one of the most successful authors of all time and at the time of his death, in Temecula, California in 1970, is said to have had 135 million copies of his books in print in America alone.

By *Erle Stanley Gardner*
(titles below include only those
published in the Murder Room)

Perry Mason series

The Case of the Sulky Girl
  (1933)
The Case of the Baited Hook
  (1940)
The Case of the Borrowed
  Brunette (1946)
The Case of the Lonely
  Heiress (1948)
The Case of the Negligent
  Nymph (1950)
The Case of the Moth-Eaten
  Mink (1952)
The Case of the Glamorous
  Ghost (1955)
The Case of the Terrified
  Typist (1956)
The Case of the Gilded Lily
  (1956)
The Case of the Lucky Loser
  (1957)
The Case of the Long-Legged
  Models (1958)
The Case of the Deadly Toy
  (1959)
The Case of the Singing Skirt
  (1959)

The Case of the Duplicate
  Daughter (1960)
The Case of the Blonde
  Bonanza (1962)

Cool and Lam series
*First published under the
pseudonym A.A. Fair*

The Bigger They Come (1939)
Turn on the Heat (1940)
Gold Comes in Bricks (1940)
Spill the Jackpot (1941)
Double or Quits (1941)
Owls Don't Blink (1942)
Bats Fly at Dusk (1942)
Cats Prowl at Night (1943)
Crows Can't Count (1946)
Fools Die on Friday (1947)
Bedrooms Have Windows
  (1949)
Some Women Won't Wait (1953)
Beware the Curves (1956)
You Can Die Laughing (1957)
Some Slips Don't Show (1957)
The Count of Nine (1958)
Pass the Gravy (1959)
Kept Women Can't Quit (1960)

Bachelors Get Lonely (1961)
Shills Can't Count Chips (1961)
Try Anything Once (1962)
Fish or Cut Bait (1963)
Up For Grabs (1964)
Cut Thin to Win (1965)
Widows Wear Weeds (1966)
Traps Need Fresh Bait (1967)

Doug Selby D.A. series

The D.A. Calls it Murder (1937)
The D.A. Holds a Candle (1938)
The D.A. Draws a Circle (1939)
The D.A. Goes to Trial (1940)
The D.A. Cooks a Goose (1942)
The D.A. Calls a Turn (1944)

The D.A. Takes a Chance (1946)
The D.A. Breaks an Egg (1949)

Terry Clane series

Murder Up My Sleeve (1937)
The Case of the Backward
  Mule (1946)

Gramp Wiggins series

The Case of the Turning Tide
  (1941)
The Case of the Smoking
  Chimney (1943)

Two Clues (two novellas) (1947)

Kept Women Can't Quit

Erle Stanley Gardner

An Orion book

Copyright © The Erle Stanley Gardner Trust 1960

This edition published by
The Orion Publishing Group Ltd
Orion House
5 Upper St Martin's Lane
London WC2H 9EA

An Hachette UK company
A CIP catalogue record for this book is available from the British Library

ISBN 978 1 4719 0910 8

www.orionbooks.co.uk

FOREWORD

WHAT are we going to do with criminals?

We have to punish people who violate the law so that the punishment may serve as a crime deterrent. But what happens to these people after they have been punished?

What are we going to do with our prisons? Are we going to maintain them as crime factories which manufacture criminals, or are we going to develop them in such a manner that we turn law violators into useful citizens?

More depends upon the answers to these questions than we realize.

After a law violator has been confined and released, what he does after his release depends to a large extent on what society has done to him while he has been incarcerated.

If society wants to use punishment as a means of 'getting even' with the criminal, the criminal is pretty apt to want to get even with society after he is released.

There aren't any easy answers, but under the guidance of James V. Bennett, Director of the Bureau of Prisons, the Federal prisons are making enormous strides.

For the past few years 1 have been in touch with Preston G. Smith, the warden of the Federal Correctional Institution at Terminal Island, San Pedro, California. I have from time to time talked with him about some of the problems of penology, and he so aptly expressed his attitude in a recent letter to me that I have asked permission to quote the following paragraphs:

I fully realize that our basic responsibility to the public and to the people committed to our care is to see that they are safely detained for the period of time prescribed by the courts. But a much more serious responsibility, in my opinion, is to help these people do something for themselves during the period of their confinement which will enable them upon release to become law-abiding and respected members of free society.

We do not claim to rehabilitate anyone. The best we can hope to do is to provide the necessary tools, encouragement and guidance to our wards to help themselves. The extent to which they avail themselves of the opportunities offered is strictly a personal matter. Each man, or woman, writes his or her own ticket. We can only cross our fingers and hope for the best.

You are, of course, familiar with what I mean by 'necessary tools.' We first try to teach fundamentals—personal grooming, clean speech, the importance of keeping their quarters and work areas clean, the satisfaction to be derived from an honest day's labor, etc. Then we go on to vocational and academic training, religious instruction, individual and group counseling, special activities such as AA, Dale Carnegie, etc. These are some of the opportunities our 'clients' have at their disposal. The extent to which they take advantage of them, as previously mentioned, is a matter for their own decision. Fortunately, an encouraging percentage *make their time serve them* and do leave the confines of prison much better equipped to assume the roles of respected members of society.

It has been my very good fortune to have been closely associated with Mr. Bennett, your good friend and our able Director, during a good part of my prison service career. Mr. Bennett's outstanding leadership and dedication to improving the lot of this unfortunate segment of our society have been a source of real inspiration to all of us who have had the opportunity to know him and to function as members of his team. We look forward with considerable apprehension to the day when he will elect to exercise his rights to a well-earned retirement. His departure will create a void which it will be most difficult to fill.

I think the above quotation comes as near to covering the situation as anything I have seen in a long time. Prisoners are human beings. You can't simply isolate them from society and then expect them to pick up their lives where they left off. A human being can't be turned on and off like an electric light or a water faucet.

The idea of a vindictive punishment is just about the worst thing that society could dream up. It may give certain individuals a brief period of sadistic satisfaction. It should be remembered, however, that the big bulk of prison inmates really want to go straight on their release. And, strangely enough, very few of them know what actually brought about the mental attitude which caused them to become law violators in the first place.

The *average* prison inmate didn't want to become a criminal any more than the drinker wants to become a drunkard.

It is high time society recognizes this fact and does something about it.

Trying to help prison inmates rehabilitate themselves and giving them the tools with which to work isn't a matter of coddling criminals; it's protecting society.

And so I dedicate this book to my friend:

Preston G. Smith, Warden at the Federal Correctional Institution at Terminal Island, California.

ERLE STANLEY GARDNER

CHAPTER ONE

THE sign that was painted on the frosted glass of the corridor door read COOL & LAM. Down below that appeared the names, B. COOL—DONALD LAM and the single word ENTER.

There was nothing about the sign on the door to indicate that B. Cool was a woman, a hundred and sixty-five pounds of greedy-eyed suspicion. Bertha Cool's shape and toughness was that of a spool of barbed wire ready for shipment f.o.b. factory.

I pushed open the door, nodded to the receptionist, walked over to the door marked DONALD LAM—PRIVATE and opened it.

Elsie Brand, my secretary, looked up from the scrapbook she was working on.

"Good morning, Donald."

I looked over her shoulder at the stuff she was pasting in the scrapbook. It was the fifth volume of unsolved cases which might at some time give us a chance to make a profit. The chances on most of these cases were one in ten thousand, but I always felt that any good detective agency should know what was cooking in the crime world.

The dress Elsie was wearing had a square cut at the throat and, as she leaned forward pasting in the clipping, I found my eyes drawn down to the line of her neck.

She felt my gaze, glanced up, laughed nervously and shifted her position. "Oh, *you!*" she said.

I looked at the piece she had been pasting in the scrapbook: the story of an audacious theft of a cool hundred thousand bucks from an armored car. It had been done so smoothly that no one knew how it had been done, where it had been done, or when it had been done. Police thought it *might* have been done at a drive-in restaurant called the Full Dinner Pail.

An intelligent fourteen-year-old boy had seen the armored truck parked at the roadside restaurant, and had noticed that a sedan was parked immediately behind the truck. A red-headed man about twenty-five was fitting a jack under the left front wheel of that sedan. The thing that

1

was odd about it was that this witness swore the car didn't have a flat tire on the left front wheel, although the man was going through all the motions of changing a tire.

The money had been in a rear compartment. It took two keys to open that compartment. One of the keys was in the hands of the driver, the other was in the pocket of the armed guard. The locks couldn't be picked.

There were always two men riding the armored trucks: the driver and the guard. They had stopped for coffee at this place, but they had carefully followed the routine of having one man remain inside the cab while the other went in and got coffee and doughnuts. Then that man came out, took his turn sitting in the cab, and the other man went in. The coffee break was a technical violation of the rules but it was a violation that the company habitually overlooked as long as one man remained in the cab of the truck.

Elsie Brand looked up at me and said, "Sergeant Sellers is closeted with Bertha Cool."

"Social, sexual or business?" I asked.

"I think it's business," she said. "I heard something over the radio when I was driving in this morning. Sellers and his partner have been working on a case and there's a rumour that fifty thousand dollars of money that was recovered is missing."

"This case?" I asked, nodding toward the clippings she had just pasted in the scrapbook.

"I wouldn't know," she said. And then added, "Bertha doesn't take me into her confidence, you know."

She changed her position slightly. The front of the dress flared out a bit and she said, "Donald, stop it."

"Stop what?"

"It wasn't made to be viewed from that angle."

"It's not an angle," I said, "it's a curve. And if it wasn't made to be viewed, why was it made so beautiful?"

She put her hand up, pushed the dress in and said, "Get your mind on business. I have an idea that Sergeant Sellers——"

She was interrupted by the ringing of the telephone.

She picked up the instrument, said, "Donald Lam's secretary," then looked at me and arched her eyebrows.

I nodded.

"Yes, Mrs. Cool," she said. "He just came in. I'll tell him."

I heard Bertha's voice, sounding raucous and metallic as it came through the receiver, saying, "Put him on. I'll tell him myself."

Elsie Brand handed me the telephone. I said, "Hello, Bertha. What's new?"

"Get in here!" Bertha snapped.

"What's the trouble?"

"Hell's to pay," she said, and hung up.

I handed the telephone back to Elsie, said, "The fried eggs must have disagreed with her this morning." I walked out of my office, across the reception room and through the door marked B. COOL—PRIVATE.

Big Bertha Cool sat in her squeaky swivel chair behind the desk. Her eyes and her diamonds were both glittering.

Police Sergeant Frank Sellers, worrying an unlit cigar like a nervous dog chewing on a rubber ball, sat in the client's chair, his jaw thrust forward as though he expected to take a punch or to give one.

"Good morning, folks," I said, making with a cheerful greeting.

Bertha said to me, "Good morning my eye! What the hell have *you* been up to?"

Frank Sellers jerked the cigar out with the first two fingers of his right hand and said, "Look here, Pint Size, if you're pulling a fast one on us, so help me God I'll break you into pieces until you look like a jigsaw puzzle. And I promise you that after I've done that no one is ever going to be able to put you back together again."

"Now what?" I asked.

"Hazel Downer," Sellers said.

I waited for him to go on but he didn't go on.

"Don't play it innocent," Sellers said, transferring the soggy cigar to his left hand as he fished in his side coat pocket with his right hand and pulled out a square of paper on which had been written in feminine handwriting "Cool and Lam," with the office address and the telephone number.

I thought for a moment there was a faint odor of heady perfume about it, but when I raised it to my nose the fresh

3

smell of damp tobacco from Sergeant Sellers' fingers over-
came the scent of perfume.

"Well?" Sellers asked.

"Well, what?" I wanted to know.

Bertha said, "You can gamble one thing, Frank. If she's
young, attractive and full of curves and has had any contact
with *this* agency, Donald is the one she saw."

Sellers nodded, reached for the slip of paper, put it back
in his pocket, shoved the cold, soggy cigar back into his
mouth, chewed on it for a minute, frowned at me ominously
and said, "She's young and full of curves—Hazel Downer,
Pint Size. *You* tell *me* about *her*."

I shook my head.

"You mean you haven't been in touch with her?" he
asked in surprise.

"Never heard of her in my life," I said.

"All right. Now look," Sellers said, "I'm going to tell
you something I've already told Bertha. It's confidential. If
I read it in the paper I'll know where it came from. Yesterday an armored truck reported a loss of a cool hundred
thousand bucks, a neat one hundred G's, all in thousand-
dollar bills.

"We got a clue from a young Eagle Scout. I'm not going
to tell you how we got it or how we ran it down, but it
pointed to a two-time loser, a red-headed sonofabitch
named Herbert Baxley, and for your information, I'm
damned apt to choke him with my two hands—I would if I
thought I could get away with it."

"We picked him up," Sellers said. "He was going places
and doing things, so we tagged along. We had a pretty good
description but we still weren't *sure*. My partner and I were
ready to close in on him but we wanted to let him lead us
around a little bit before we made the pinch.

"This guy had been eating at the Full Dinner Pail.
That's a drive-in where they have some of the most cur-
vaceous cuties in town. When the weather's hot they come
out in shorts that leave nothing whatever to the imagination. When the weather's cool they have slacks and sweaters
that fit them like the skin on a sausage and leave but little
to the imagination.

"They do lots of business—too damn much business.

4

We're going to look into the place on a morals charge one of these days and we may knock it over. But the point is that quite a few regular customers drop in there for coffee breaks. That was where this armored truck had been pulling in almost every day for the last month while the two drivers took turns drinking coffee and eating doughnuts and getting an eyeful. There's both curb and counter service.

"We have reason to believe that's where someone got into the back of the armored truck with a set of duplicate keys and grabbed the hundred G's.

"Anyhow, while we're tailing this character Baxley, he goes into the joint and orders some hamburgers to take out. He ordered two hamburgers, one with everything, one with everything except onions. They gave them to him in a paper bag. Then he went out to his car and waited for this dame he was to meet to show up.

"She didn't show. He looked at his watch several times and was mad. After a while he ate *both* hamburgers—the two of them, you understand, the one with onions and the one without. Then he threw the napkin and the paper bag in the garbage, wiped his hands, got back in his car and drove off down the street. It's a cinch some dame was to join him and they were going places with two hamburgers. The dame didn't want onions. He did. He wouldn't have ordered one with and one without if he'd been intending to eat both of them. So the way we look at it something must have made this dame suspicious and she stood him up.

"Anyhow, we tailed along behind Baxley. He left this drive-in and went to a service station where there was a telephone booth. He parked his car and went into the booth. We carry a pretty damned good pair of binoculars for situations of that sort and I focused the binoculars on the telephone and was able to pick up the number he was dialing. It was Columbine 6–9403.

"I didn't want to miss that number he was calling, so we may have been parked a little closer than we should have. The guy was just starting to talk on the phone when he happened to look over his shoulder right square into the binoculars I was holding on him. I still don't know whether he saw us or not but I made the sort of blunder that's mighty easy to make. Those were nine-power binoculars and sharp as a tack. We were seventy-five feet away in a parked automobile, but when he looked up and looked right in my eyes as I was looking through those binoculars it looked just the way it would look if a guy eight feet away had looked up and suddenly seen me. I yelled to my partner, 'Okay, he's made us. After him!'

"We boiled out of the car. Well, if he hadn't seen us before, he sure as hell saw us then. He tore out of the booth, leaving the receiver dangling, and jumped into his car. Before he could get it started we had our guns on him and he didn't dare to make a play for it, so he stuck his hands up in the air.

"We frisked him and found a gun, and we also found keys to his apartment, his address and all of that stuff, and by the time we worked him over he admitted he was a two-time loser.

"My partner drove the squad car behind us. I got in his car, put the cuffs on him and drove. We didn't want to take a chance on leaving anything unsearched, so before we booked him we stopped by his apartment. We found a locked suitcase. I picked the lock and there were fifty G's inside, a cool fifty thousand bucks, exactly one half of the loot. I took the damned apartment to pieces and I couldn't find any more.

"So we took this guy and the fifty G's down to Headquarters and what do you think the sonofabitch said after we got there?"

"That you'd gone south with fifty G's," I said.

Sellers chewed on the cigar, then took it out of his mouth as though he didn't like the taste of it and nodded moodily. "That's *exactly* what he said. What's more, the Colter-Craig Casualty Company, that handles the insurance on everything shipped in the armored trucks of the Specie and Securities Transfer Company, sort of halfway believe the sonofabitch. It was a damn good thing for him he waited to say it until he got to Headquarters or he wouldn't be as smart-looking as he is now.

"All right, you know what that means and I know what it means. It means that he had a partner who was in on the thing with him and he split the swag two ways. Then he blew the whistle on us when we only found half of it.

6

"Okay, we had an answer of our own for that. We went out and started looking for the partner. Naturally the first clue we had was this telephone number, Columbine 6-9403.

"That's a private phone. It's in Apartment Seven A at the Laramie Apartments. It's a high-class dump. The owner of Apartment Seven A is a cute trick named Hazel Downer. Hazel Downer has lots of this and that and these and those. By the time we got there she was packing up, getting ready to take a run-out powder. We nailed her before she could get anywhere. She claims that Herbert Baxley had been making passes at her but that she wouldn't have any and that from time to time he'd called her; that he'd found out her telephone number somehow but that she'd never given it to him.

"Now then, we finally got a warrant and frisked her place, and I mean we *really* frisked it. All we found was this thing in her purse, that slip of paper with the name 'Cool and Lam' written on it.

"Now, the way I put two and two together, Hazel Downer was in on this thing with Herbert Baxley. She had managed to get hold of the keys to the armored car, had duplicates made and Baxley pulled the job."

"She worked at the Full Dinner Pail?" I asked.

"No, she didn't," Sergeant Sellers said. "If she had, she'd have been in the can right now. But she'd been a car hop once, she'd been a secretary for a while, and then she had suddenly become fairly affluent. For the last few months she's been living in this swank apartment and she hasn't been working. We can't find out where the man is that's keeping her. All we know is his name, Standley Downer. She's posing as his wife. My best guess is she's just a pick-up. Somehow she managed to get word to this Downer guy, or someone tipped him off and he's crawled into a hole and pulled the hole in after him.

"We can't get a single damn thing on this Hazel Downer except that Baxley was calling her up from a phone booth. Well, we can't hold her on that and if she got really nasty about it she could probably raise hell over the search-warrant business. I signed that affidavit myself. I was so damn certain we'd find the other half of the loot cached in her apartment that I stuck my neck way, way out. Either she or Standley Downer is Baxley's partner but we're going to have a hell of a time proving it—now.

"Now then, Pint Size, I'm just going to tell you that this girl is hotter than a stove lid. If you so much as give her the time of day we'll have your license and——"

Bertha Cool's telephone jangled.

Bertha ignored it for a couple of rings but the bell had thrown Sellers off his stride and he looked up, waiting for Bertha to answer it.

Bertha picked up the telephone, said, "Hello," then frowned and said, "He's busy now, Elsie. It can wait, can't it?"

Bertha listened for a moment, hesitated, then said, "Well, all right, I'll put him on."

Bertha turned to me. "Elsie says it's something important."

I picked up the telephone and Elsie Brand, talking in a very low voice so that what she said couldn't be picked up by anyone else in the room, said, "There's a Mrs. Hazel Downer here to see you, Donald. She looks like a million dollars and she says it's important and highly confidential."

I said, "He'll have to wait until I——"

"It's a *her*," Elsie interrupted.

"I said *he'll* just have to wait. I'm in an important conference in Bertha's office." I hung up the phone.

Bertha's greedy little eyes snapped. "If he's a good client, don't take any chance on losing him, Donald," she said. "Sergeant Sellers only wanted to find out whether this Hazel Downer had been in touch with us. He's said everything he wanted to say."

Sergeant Sellers took the cigar out of his mouth, looked around and said, "Why the hell don't you keep spittoons in this joint, Bertha?"

He deposited the remains of the soggy, chewed-up cigar in Bertha's ash tray.

"We don't keep spittoons," Bertha said. "This is a high-class place. Take that goddam thing out of here. It stinks up the office. I don't like it.... All right, Donald, Sergeant Sellers has told you what he wanted to say. Go ahead and do whatever it is this man wants done."

I said to Sellers, "He ordered two sandwiches, one with onions, one without?"

"That's right."

"And then ate them both?"

"That's what I said."

"Then he must have become suspicious *after* he'd ordered the sandwiches and *before* they were delivered to him."

"*He* wasn't suspicious," Sellers exploded. "It was the jane who was to join him. She stood him up. That's why he ate both sandwiches."

I said, "Then why not phone her from the drive-in? Why would he leave the place and *then* stop to telephone?"

Sellers said, "He wanted to find out why she hadn't joined him. He didn't know he was being tailed."

"But he did see the binoculars?" I asked.

"I thought he did."

"And went into a panic?"

"I ranked it," Sellers admitted. "I sprung the trap too soon. He may not have seen the binoculars, but he seemed to be looking right into my eyes."

I said, "Perhaps you missed something, Sergeant. I don't think he'd have let you watch him telephone if——"

Sergeant Sellers interrupted me. "Now look," he warned, "you're one damn smart customer. I'm not underestimating you one bit. My neck's stuck out on this thing but I don't need your help, and I don't want your hindrance. Just lay off—understand?"

Bertha said, "You don't need to talk to Donald like that, Frank."

"The hell I don't," Sellers said. "This guy is too damned clever to suit me. He's smart. He's too damned smart. He thinks he's even smarter."

I said, "I didn't give *you* as a character reference to anybody that I know of. Now, if you'll excuse me, I'm busy. We have a living to make and we can't make it just sitting around listening to people making threats."

I walked out of Bertha Cool's office, hurried across the reception room down to my private office and opened the door.

Elsie Brand jerked her thumb toward the inner office and said, "In there." And then added, "Boy-oh-boy! This one is a knock-out!"

I handed Elsie a key.

"What's this?" she said.

"The key to the men's washroom down the hall," I said. "Take her down there, get inside and bolt the door."

"What?"

"You heard me."

"Why down there? Why not to the ladies' room? Why not——?"

"Down there," I said. "Get started."

I opened the door to the inner office and walked in.

Hazel Downer was sitting with her knees crossed, facing the door. The pose had been carefully studied with just the proper amount of cheesecake and then perhaps because she'd been afraid I wouldn't take sufficient notice she had added a little to the visible nylon. It looked great.

I said, "Hello, Hazel. I'm Donald Lam and you're in a jam. This is Elsie Brand, my secretary. She's taking you down the hall. Go with her and wait."

I turned to Elsie. "I'll give you my code knock on the door."

"Come along, Hazel," Elsie said.

"Where is this place?" Hazel asked, somewhat suspiciously.

"It's the washroom," Elsie said.

"Well, what do you know!" Hazel said, and got up off the chair, holding her chest out, and accompanied Elsie out of the office without looking back to see if I was watching her hips.

She didn't have to. She was dressed so it would have been an impossibility not to have watched.

I sat down in my office swivel chair and started doodling on paper.

It was about a minute and a half before the door was jerked open by Sergeant Sellers. Bertha was looking apprehensively over his shoulder.

"Where's your man?" Sellers asked.

"What man?"

"Your client."

"Oh," I said, "it didn't amount to anything. It was a guy with a small collection job."

"Donald," Bertha said, "you can't turn down all those small jobs. I've told you time and time again that there's money in those small things."

"Not in this one," I said. "The bill was only a hundred and twenty-five dollars and he didn't know where the debtor was living. We'd have to find the debtor first and then we'd have to collect."

"Well, we could have at least looked into it," Bertha said. "You can get those things on a fifty percent commission and——"

"He told me twenty-five was his limit, so I told him to beat it."

Bertha heaved a sigh. "Can you imagine the way these bastards want to chisel these days?"

Sellers looked around the office. "Where's your secretary?"

I jerked my head. "Down the hall, I guess. Why? You want her?"

"No," Sellers said, "I'm just checking."

He jerked the soggy cigar out of his mouth and dumped it in my ash tray. I let it stay there because the odor of moist tobacco served somewhat to kill the perfume which had emanated from Hazel Downer. Sellers' nose was too paralyzed with the cigar odor for him to notice, but I thought Bertha had given a suspicious sniff when Sellers had first jerked the door open.

"All right, Frank," Bertha Cool said. "You know we won't try to cut any corners."

"I know *you* won't," Sellers said, "but I'm not so sure about Pint Size here."

I said, "Look, Sergeant, if there's fifty grand in it, why don't you encourage her to come and see us and see what she has to say? We might be able to help you."

"You might and again you might not," Sellers said. "If you ever tied up with her she'd be *your* client and you'd be representing *her* interests."

"All right. What are her interests?" I asked.

"To get away with the fifty G's."

I shook my head and said. "Not if it's hot. We could

help her make a deal with the police. Perhaps the armored car outfit would give us five G's as a reward. Then you'd be off the spot and she could be in the clear."

Sellers said, "When I need your help I'll ask for it."

"All right, keep your shirt on," I told him.

"What was an armored truck doing with a hundred one-thousand dollar bills?" I asked.

Sellers said, "The stuff had been ordered by the Merchants' Manufacturers and Seamans' National. They tell us the order came from a depositor and won't go any further than that. We think it was a big bookmaking concern, but we can't prove it. Anyhow, the money was in the truck, and now it's gone. . . . You got any ideas?"

"None you'd want," I said. "Or are you asking for help now?"

"Go to hell," Sellers said, and walked out.

Bertha waited until the door had closed, then said, "Don't try to handle Sergeant Sellers that way, Donald. You deliberately made him mad."

"So what?" I said. "Here we are fooling around with fifty grand in money and Sergeant Sellers is in a spot. Suppose *we* can solve his problem, recover fifty G's for the insurance company and cut ourselves a piece of cake."

Bertha's eyes glittered greedily for a minute, then she shook her head apprehensively. "We can't do it."

"Why not?"

"Because they'd nail us to the cross, that's why."

"For what?"

"For compounding a felony, being an accessory after the fact, and——"

"*You're* going to tell *me* about the law?" I asked.

"You're damn right," she said. "I'm *telling* you about the law."

I said, "I know a little law myself, Bertha. Suppose Sellers is barking up the wrong tree. Suppose this man Baxley had just been trying to date this jane, but suppose she knows something about him. Suppose if we treated her nice she could give us a clue?"

Bertha thought it over, then shook her head, but this time the shake wasn't quite so emphatic.

"Sergeant Sellers can't tell us what to do and what not to

do," I said. "He's got a theory, that's all. What has he got to tie it to? Nothing except a telephone number."

"With the whole damn Police Department back of him," Bertha said. "When you get to tangling with those boys they can be tough."

"I don't intend to tangle with them," I said.

"Well, what do you intend to do?"

"Run my own business in my own way," I told her.

Bertha slammed out of the office.

I waited two minutes, then opened the door and stepped out to the hall.

Sergeant Sellers was standing by the elevators.

"What's the matter, Sergeant?" I asked. "The elevators on strike?"

"No," he said, "I'm just keeping an eye on you, wise guy. There's a gleam in your eye I don't like. Where you headed?"

"Down to the john," I said, jangling my keys. "You want to come?"

"Go to hell," he told me.

I walked down the corridor. Sergeant Sellers followed me with his eyes.

I pretended to be inserting a key in the door while I tapped my code signal on the panels. I heard the bolt move on the inside. The door opened a bit and Elsie Brand's frightened voice said, "Donald?"

I said, "Okay, baby, stand back," and pushed my way into the room, closed the door behind me and shot the bolt.

"Well, I *like* this," Hazel Downer said.

"What's wrong with it?" I asked.

"The fixtures."

"I didn't have time to change them," I said. "Now look, you're hotter than a stove lid. Sergeant Sellers of the Police Department is waiting out there in the hall."

"That so-and-so!" Hazel Downer said. "What right has he got to start pushing me around? I haven't done anything."

Elsie Brand looked at me with wide eyes.

"All right," I said to Hazel, "what do you want?"

She looked me over. "I want some service but I don't

13

want it here——and I don't know whether you can give it to me."

"Why not?"

"You're not the sort of man I expected."

"What kind did you expect?"

"A big-shouldered, two-fisted fighter," she said.

"Mr. Lam fights with his brains," Elsie told her, rushing to my defense.

Hazel Downer looked around at the "fixtures" and said, "So it seems."

"All right," I told her. "There's no harm done. I'm walking out. I'll decoy Frank Sellers down to the sidewalk, then you girls get out of here. You go back to the office, Elsie. Hazel can take care of herself. When you get to the street, Hazel, Frank Sellers will be there waiting for you. You're going to see a lot of Frank Sellers."

Hazel Downer looked frightened. "I don't know anything about *his* fifty grand," she said. "This Baxley was a torpedo that was on the make. I don't even know how he got my telephone number."

I stretched and yawned. "Why tell me? You don't like me, remember?"

Her eyes sized me up. "Maybe I could like you——under other circumstances and in a different environment."

"This is the environment we're forced to use at the moment. What did you want?"

"I wanted you to find a man."

"Standley Downer."

"And who's Standley Downer?"

"He's the so-and-so who skipped out with my dough."

"Any relative?"

"I said yes to the guy."

"Where?"

"In front of an altar."

"Then what?"

"I thought you were smart," she said.

"He means with the money," Elsie said.

"That's what *I* meant," Hazel said.

"Where did you get the money?" I asked.

"From an uncle."

"How much?"

"Sixty grand."

"After taxes?"

"After taxes and attorneys' fees. That was net to me."

"Any way of proving it?"

"Of course. There are court records."

"They'll be checked," I told her.

She bit her lip.

"All right," I said. "What's wrong?"

"There aren't any court records. My uncle was what they call a rugged individualist. He did business on a cash basis. He cheated on the income tax. He had sixty grand salted away in a deposit box. When he knew it was the end of the road for him he sent for me."

"Now then," I said, "all you need to tell me is that he had this sixty grand in thousand-dollar bills and that he gave it all to you."

"That's exactly what happened."

"And you didn't dare to deposit it in a bank because the income-tax people would want to know where all the money came from, so you hid it someplace and then you married Standley Downer and Downer wondered where your money was coming from and you wouldn't tell him so he got smart and finally found where you had hidden it and took the boodle and departed."

"That's right."

"So," I said, "you want me to find him. Now, if you're lying and this money represents your share of the fruits of the robbery of that armored truck I'd go to prison as being an accessory after the fact and be there for probably fifteen years. On the other hand, if your story is true and I found the money I'd be accessory after the fact to income-tax evasion and would probably get off with about five years. No, thank you, I don't want any of it."

"Wait a minute," she said. "I'll come clean."

"Go ahead."

"You find my husband and the money and *then* I'll prove I have the title."

I said, "When I find Standley Downer, what's going to keep him from telling us to go chase ourselves?"

"I am."

"How?"

15

"I have something on him."

"This fits into a beautiful picture——" I said, "black-mail, cheating the income tax and compounding a felony. I don't like it."

"You get fifty bucks a day and a bonus depending on what I get back."

"How big a bonus?"

"That depends on how long it takes."

"Twenty percent."

"All right, twenty percent."

Elsie Brand looked at me pleadingly. Her eyes were begging me not to have anything to do with it.

"We'd need a retainer," I said.

"How much?"

"A thousand."

"Are you crazy? I haven't got it."

'What do you have?"

"Five hundred is every cent I have."

"Where?"

She put a foot on one of the fixtures, elevated her skirt and took a plastic envelope from the top of her stocking. She pulled back the flap of the envelope. There were five one-hundred-dollar bills inside.

"Have any trouble changing it?" I asked.

"Changing what?"

"The thousand-dollar bill."

"Go to hell," she said. 'Do you want this, or don't you?"

I said, "Let me tell you something, sister. If you're mixed up in that armored car business I'm going to turn you in. If you're lying I'll sell you down the river. If you're telling me the truth, I'm going to find Standley Downer."

"Fair enough," she said, "you find him and then we'll talk turkey, but you'll have to find him before he's spent it all."

"How long has he been gone?"

"A week."

"You got a picture?"

She opened her purse, took out a wallet, extracted a picture, handed it to me.

"What color hair?"

16

"Dark."

"Eyes?"

"Blue."

"Weight?"

"A hundred and seventy."

"Height?"

"Six feet, even."

"Age?"

"Twenty-nine."

"Disposition?"

"It varies."

"Emotional?"

"Yes."

"Have you been married before?" I asked.

"If it's any of your business, yes."

"How many times?"

"Twice."

"Had he been married before?"

"Once."

"You're quite a dish," I said, looking her over.

She said, "Am I really?" She ran her hands over her curves. "Why," she said in exaggerated surprise, "thank you for telling me, Mr. Lam. *I* hadn't noticed."

I said, "We don't have time for wisecracks or sarcasm. You're a dish."

"All right, I'm a dish, so what?"

"Your husband didn't leave you unless he had something especially attractive. Who was it?"

"Wasn't the dough enough?"

I shook my head. "Quit stalling. Who's the other girl?"

"Evelyn Ellis."

"Now then," I said, "if you tell me Evelyn works at the Full Dinner Pail, I'll have heard everything."

"But she does," she said. "That's where my husband met her."

I put the five hundred dollars in my pocket. "Okay," I said, "this is where I came in."

Elsie Brand grabbed my arm. "*Please* don't, Donald."

I said, "It's an occupational hazard, Elsie."

Hazel Downer was immediately suspicious. "What's a hazard? What are you two signaling about?"

I said, "Never mind that. Describe Evelyn."

"Red-head, wide innocent-looking blue eyes, twenty-three, a hundred and seventeen pounds; thirty-six, twenty-four, thirty-six."

"What's she got you haven't got?"

"She didn't ask me to be present when my husband was taking inventory."

"You seem to be pretty familiar with the dimensions."

"Why not? She had everything published when she was Miss American Hardware at the Hardware Dealers' Convention last year."

"What was she doing in hardware?"

"She wasn't in hardware. She was a bookkeeper for an importing company."

"What was she doing as a car hop?"

"That was after the hardware. She was looking for impressionable men who had, or could get, money. She found Standley. She's retired now."

"You have any idea where they are now?"

"If I did I wouldn't be paying you."

"What am I to do if and when I find them?"

"Just tell me."

I turned to Elsie. "After I leave, wait three minutes," I said. "Open the door a crack to see if anyone's in the corridor. If the coast is clear, go back to the office. If Bertha wants to know anything, act like a clam."

I swung back to face Hazel Downer. "You follow Elsie out," I said. "Take the elevator to the main floor. Go down the block to the big department store. The ladies' room has two entrances. Go in one and out the other. Be sure you aren't followed.

"Every day at noon leave your apartment. Try not to be followed. Go to a pay phone booth and call Elsie in my office. Make your voice as harsh as you can. Say this is Abigail Smythe and tell Elsie to be sure the last name is spelled with a *y* and an *e* and where is the deadbeat you married I'm supposed to be locating for you.

"Elsie will tell you where to meet me if I have anything new. When you dial the number, be sure no one is watching.

"You got all that straight?"

She nodded.

I opened the door and walked out.

Sergeant Sellers was halfway down the corridor coming toward me.

"It takes you a long time," he said.

"Bertha's time," I pointed out. "That's the only way I can get even with her. Thank you for your interest in what I do."

"Where are you going now?"

"Out."

"I'll go with you."

"Sure thing. Come along."

He rode down in the elevator with me.

"I wouldn't want you to get any ideas," he said. "Remember, smart guy, I'm going to bust this case wide open. Do you get me? *I'm* going to bust it wide open."

"That's nice," I said.

"I don't need any help."

"I know," I told him. "In the bright lexicon of youth there is no such word as fail."

"What the hell's a lexicon?" he asked.

"A Greek dictionary," I told him.

"Someday," he told me, "you're going to get hurt."

"I've already been hurt."

"Worse," he said.

I saw him looking at the cigar stand.

"Come on down the block with me," I said. "There's a good-looking blonde at the cigar counter down there. I'm going to shake dice with her for the cigars. I'll give you a couple."

"You and your women," he said.

"You and your cigars," I told him.

He walked along with me. I stuck the house for cigars. I gave him half. I hated to contribute them but I couldn't afford to have him see Hazel Downer when she left the building. Sometimes you have to give the other guy the breaks.

CHAPTER TWO

THE public relations counsel who had engineered publicity for the National Hardware Association was Jasper Diggs Calhoun. Everything about his offices was arranged to impress visitors with the idea that they were entering the presence of a DYNAMIC PERSONALITY.

The attractive secretary, with lots of curves showing through a tight-fitting dress, had an expression of demure innocence on her face which had been carefully cultivated. It made her look as though she had no idea the curves were showing.

"Can you tell me what you wished to discuss with Mr. Calhoun, Mr. Lam?" she asked, her wide blue eyes looking at me with naïve innocence.

"An interesting problem in post-public relations," I said.

"*Post*-public relations?"

"That's right."

"Can you explain what you mean by that?"

"Certainly," I said, "I can explain it in a very few words —to Mr. Calhoun."

I gave her a smile.

She got up from behind the desk and walked around it so that I could see how her dress fitted in the back. It fitted. She vanished through a door marked J. D. CALHOUN— PRIVATE, and within a few minutes emerged to say, "You may go in, Mr. Lam. You have no appointment but Mr. Calhoun will endeavor to shuffle his other appointments so he can see you. He has just returned from luncheon and he has several appointments; however, he'll see you."

"Thank you," I said, and walked in.

Calhoun sat behind his desk, leaning slightly forward, an attitude of dynamic energy about him. His lips were carefully held in a straight line. The small mustache had been trimmed so that it emphasized the look of determination which was as synthetic as the expression of innocence on the face of his secretary.

He was broad-shouldered, somewhere in the thirties, with dark hair, dark eyebrows and piercing gray eyes.

"*Mr. Lam!*" he exclaimed, getting up and extending his arm as though he was shooting his hand at a mark.

I put my hand in his and arched the knuckles so that his squeeze didn't make me wince. I could tell he was a chronic hand squeezer. It showed his dynamic personality.

"How are you, Mr. Lam? Sit down. My secretary said you wanted to discuss a problem in post-public relations."

"That's right."

"What is it?"

I said, "You public relations men do a lot of thinking. You dream up some terrific ideas. The ideas are used and then forgotten. That's a waste of good material. In many instances there are opportunities to get good publicity out of things which might be termed the aftermath."

"Such as what?" he asked.

"Oh, generally," I said, waving my hand around the office and looking at the photographs on the wall, "any of your ideas. Now, here's something interesting. This is quite a photograph."

Calhoun yawned and said, "*You* may think so, but in this business, bathing beauties and models are a dime a dozen. We use cheesecake in our business."

"Just why do you use cheesecake?" I asked.

He said, "Look, I'm too busy to give you lessons in the public relations business. Generally, if we're selling something that has no eye appeal we try to attract the reader's interest in terms of cheesecake.

"That's why you see new models of automobiles photographed alongside girls in bathing suits or good-looking models with tight-fitting skirts and nylons. We have them by the dozen. That particular photograph you're looking at shows the contestants who were vying to win the thousand-dollar cash prize and the title of Miss American Hardware. That was publicity for the hardware convention at New Orleans a few months ago. I handled all their publicity."

"They're good-looking babes," I said.

"Yeah," he repeated in a bored voice, "they're good-looking babes—so what?"

"Who won?"

"Contestant Number Six," he said.

"Now, there's something that would be interesting," I

said. "That's what I mean by post-public relations. I'll bet Contestant Number Six would interest the American public. She was a girl working as a waitress someplace or——"

"She was a bookkeeper in an important house," he interrupted.

"All right," I said, "she was a bookkeeper. She had great beauty but no one recognized it. She was doing humdrum daily tasks, and then she heard of a contest for the queen of the National Hardware Association. Timidly she typed out an application. She found out it would be necessary to appear in a bathing suit. She hesitated for a while, and then decided to go ahead with it. She——"

"You said she *timidly* typed out an application?" he interrupted.

"That's right."

"Not that babe," he told me. "As I remember it, she was the one who suspected one of the other girls had padding in her bathing suit and suggested that the judging should be done in such a manner that the judges would be satisfied no artificial aids to beauty were being used.... My secretary can tell you a lot more about her. I don't remember too much of the details. It was just another contest, and, frankly, we get damn good and tired of them."

"I know," I said, "but think of the follow-up—that's what I'm coming to. She won. The elation, the——"

"The cash," he said dryly.

"All right, the cash. And all the notoriety, the publicity, the chance to go to Hollywood. I suppose you provided for some sort of a screen test?"

"Oh, sure," he said, "that's what makes the thing attractive to the public. There's a photograph over there on the other wall showing me handing her the thousand-dollar check, the contract for a screen test, the television appearance as Miss American Hardware on a national hookup ... it's all of a routine buildup these days. The newspapers will give you space on it—if they're hard up for news."

I walked over to the other side of the room and looked at the photograph of Jasper Diggs Calhoun trying not to look bored and the winner looking up at him with soulful eyes. She'd taken a full breath and pushed her chest out and her stomach in. The bathing suit fitted her like the skin on a

22

sausage. Down underneath was a caption: "Evelyn Ellis acclaimed Queen of American Hardware Wholesalers' Convention."

"You're not in hardware?" I asked Calhoun.

He shook his head. "I'm in public relations."

"I should think that the presentation would have been made by one of the officials of the Hardware Association."

"That shows all you know about it," he said. "Those birds are married. Their wives don't like to have them photographed in public with bathing cuties."

"Aren't you married?"

"Sure, but that's my business. My wife understands. I can show you a thousand photographs taken of me and cheesecake."

"Then the hardware executives keep themselves aloof from the queen?" I asked.

"Don't be silly," he said. "They're not photographed with her in public, but they brush up against her, they let their hands slide along the curves of the bathing suit. Some of them are always patting her on the fanny and telling her to be a good girl. What the hell! That's part of the game. That's what she got the thousand bucks for; that, and the opportunity to show off."

"Well," I said, "she could be great material. Think of what happened afterward—I suppose she attracted a lot of attention on television?"

"My God, but you're naïve," Calhoun said.

"Well, what did happen?" I asked.

Calhoun said, "You're taking up a lot of my time. Do I get anything out of this, Lam?"

"Sure you do," I said. "If I can make a story out of this I'll write it from the angle of the public relations expert. All this cheesecake thrills the public, but with us it's a dime a dozen and——"

"Now, wait a minute," he interrupted hastily. "Don't pull *that* line. That disillusions the public. In public relations we don't want the public disillusioned. Now, you just back up and begin all over. You sketch me as the enthusiastic guy who likes to see these girls make good, who has an eye for beauty—professionally, of course. I can see a girl as a bookkeeper or as a waitress or an usherette or something of that sort and tell right away if she's got what it takes. I am as thrilled as the public is with the romantic opportunities for discovery and advancement. They're Cinderellas. I'm a fairy godmother. I wave the wand of publicity and, presto, they're made. That's the kind of publicity I want."

"I see your point," I said. "Where is this woman now? What's her name?"

"It's on the caption there," he said. "Evelyn something. I remember I had to make the check over because she spelled it with a *y*."

"Evelyn Ellis," I said, reading from the photograph. "Where is she now?"

"How would I know? The last I saw of her personally was when I gave her this check."

"May I ask your secretary? Would she have the address?"

"Oh, I'll dig it out for you. I'll find it."

He opened his desk, rummaged around among some cards, then opened another drawer, looked in some books, finally went to still a third drawer and pulled out a notebook.

"Evelyn Ellis," he said, "at the time of her last television appearance was living at the Breeze-Mount Hotel."

"I take it that after the Hardware Convention you dropped this bit of cheesecake and started thinking up other publicity stunts."

That got a sparkle of response. "You've said it, Lam. We have to keep coming up with new ideas like this and this and this . . ."

He raised his right hand and snapped his fingers every time he said "this."

I nodded. "I might be able to make quite a story out of that."

"Would it do me any good?"

"Would it do you any harm?" I asked.

"No, I don't suppose so."

"Publicity," I said, "is always good."

"Well, this sort of publicity *might* not be too good— particularly if she isn't happy or prosperous or . . . you know how it is with a girl of that sort. She expects to crash Hollywood just because she has a good figure and has won a contest. The woods are full of those girls. Usually they can't stand the disappointment. After they've had the glamour and the adulation it's difficult for them to settle down to routine work."

"How about looking her up and letting me know where she is now?"

He said, "I'll have to think this one over. Give me a ring tomorrow."

"I'll do that," I promised. "Perhaps we can help each other."

We shook hands again.

I went out and the automatic door-closing device clicked the door shut behind me.

I turned to the secretary, looked her over and said, "How in the world does it happen they don't use *you*?"

"For what?" she asked.

"For Miss American Hardware at the convention of the National Hardware Association," I said. "Good heavens, how did they pick Evelyn Ellis when *you* were around?"

She lowered her eyelids. "Mr. Calhoun never uses the pesonnel in the office."

I looked her over again appraisingly. She registered becoming modesty under my glance.

"Where's Evelyn now?" I asked casually.

She made a little gesture. "For a while she was on Cloud Seven, ringing up and wanting help getting bookings as a model, wanting us to help her crash the movies. She had a few television appearances and she thought she was the belle of the ball. She quit her job, couldn't get up until one or two o'clock in the afternoon, spent a couple of hours a day in the beauty parlors."

I nodded sympathetically. "I know the type."

"Then she got a job as a car hop somewhere, and more recently she skipped out with a married man."

"Where's she living?" I asked.

"She *was* living at the Breeze-Mount Hotel," she said.

"Look," I said, taking out a ten-dollar bill. "You've got lots of pictures of her. I want some. I haven't time to hunt her up and then hire a photographer. How about it?"

She eyed the ten, hesitated.

"Does Mr. Calhoun know you are asking me for these pictures?"

"Will Mr. Calhoun know I gave you ten bucks?"

She took the ten.

She went to a filing cabinet, looked at a card, went to another cabinet and took out some photos. She ran through the photos, found two that were duplicates and handed me the copies.

"Will these do?"

I looked at the photos and whistled.

"Evidently those will do," she said acidly.

"I was surprised," I said. "Those other pictures Mr. Calhoun has in his office weren't so revealing."

"Those were for the newspapers," she said. "These were for the nominating committee."

I said, "If you ever try out for a contest I'd sure like to know how to get on the nominating committee. How would I go about it?"

She looked me over, smiled. "Why not start your own contest?"

Before I could answer a buzzer sounded.

The secretary flashed me a dazzling smile. "Excuse me, Mr. Lam," she said. "Mr. Calhoun wants me."

I didn't go out until after she had walked around the desk, so that she could see I was standing there to watch her as she walked.

She looked back over her shoulder just before she opened the door and flashed me another dazzling smile.

I walked out, looking at the photographs. They bore the signature of some Japanese photographer and on the back was the stamp, HAPPY DAZE CAMERA CO.

The Happy Daze Camera Company had a San Francisco address.

CHAPTER THREE

THE telephone directory listed the Breeze-Mount Hotel as an apartment hotel. I called the hotel and asked for the manager. The woman who was on the phone said, "This is the manager, Mrs. Marlene Charlotte."

I said, "I'm inquiring for a Miss Evelyn Ellis. Can you tell me if she has her own phone or——"

"She has her own phone, which is still in the apartment, but she vacated the apartment yesterday afternoon, and didn't even do me the courtesy of calling on me," she said. "She moved out and left me a note stating that her rent was paid up until the first and I could rent the apartment immediately."

"You don't know where she went?"

"I don't know where she went. I don't know why she went. I don't know who she went with. Who is this talking?"

"Mr. Smith," I said. "I hoped I could catch her before she left. I'm sorry."

I hung up.

I called the office and asked to talk with Elsie Brand.

"Hi, Elsie," I said. "Want to do something for me?"

"It depends on how wild it is."

"This one is *really* wild," I said. "You have to compromise your good name."

"Oh, is that all?"

"That's not all," I said, "that's just the first step."

"How come?"

I said, "I'll be sitting in the agency heap outside of the Breeze-Mount Apartment Hotel. That's at the corner of Breeze-Mount Drive and Thirty-third Avenue. Take a taxi and come out there. Take the signet ring off your right hand, put it on the ring finger of your left hand, turn it around so it looks like a wedding ring when someone is looking at the back of your hand. Make it just as fast as you can."

"Donald, I wish you wouldn't do this," she said.

"I know," I told her, "but's done. Will you or do I have

to get a woman operative and have Bertha screaming about the expenses?"

"Better get the woman operative. Bertha likes to scream."

"Okay," I said. "This gal is going to be my wife for a while. If the operative sues the agency for——"

"Say, what *is* this?" she interrupted.

"A very intimate, interesting job."

"All right, I'll help. You want me there right away?"

"Just as soon as you can make it. Anybody watching the office?"

"Not that I know of."

"Haven't you seen anything more of Sergeant Sellers?"

"No, Donald, a letter was delivered here by special messenger. It's addressed to you and marked personal and important."

"Bring it along and come on out," I said.

I hung up the telephone and called the Colter-Craig Casualty Company.

When the operator at their switchboard answered, I said, "Who's in charge of the investigation on this armored car business?"

"I think," she said, "you should talk with Mr. George Abner. Just a moment and I'll connect you."

A moment later a man's voice said, "Hello. George B. Abner talking."

"You in charge of that armored car loss?" I asked.

"I am the investigator," he said cautiously. "Who is this talking?"

"Mile," I said.

"You mean Mr. Miles?"

"I said 'Mile.' Do you know how many feet are in a mile?"

"Certainly."

"How many?"

"What is this, a gag?"

"Remember the number," I said. "Five thousand, two hundred and eighty. If I call you in the future I'll simply refer to the number—five thousand, two hundred and eighty. Now then, if I can get you all or part of the fifty grand that's missing and hand it to you on a silver platter, what is there in it for me?"

"I don't do that sort of business over the telephone," he said. "And for your information, Mr. Mile, we don't compound felonies."

"No one's asking you to compound a felony," I said. "You're facing a loss of fifty grand. What's it worth to cut it down?"

"If the offer is legitimate," he said, "our company has always been generous in the matter of rewards, but we certainly don't discuss things of this sort over the telephone in this manner."

"What do you mean, being most generous? Fifty percent?" I asked.

"Heavens, no!" he said. "That would be suicidal. We might go to twenty percent."

"Twenty-five," I said.

"If you have something definite to offer," he said, "we'll be glad to discuss the matter with you."

"I'm making a definite offer," I said. "Twenty-five percent of whatever is recovered."

"If and when anything is recovered," he said, "I would certainly not recommend going above twenty percent. That represents the highest we go as a matter of policy. Usually we give rewards of around ten percent."

"Perhaps that's why you have such high losses," I said. "Remember the name, and above all, the code number five thousand, two hundred and eighty."

I hung up, got in the agency heap and drove to the Breeze-Mount Apartment Hotel.

I had to wait about ten minutes before the taxicab deposited Elsie Brand.

I paid off the cab and sent him on his way.

"Come on, Elsie," I said, "we're going in."

"What are we going to do?" she asked.

"Rent an apartment," I said. "Get friendly with the manager. Be nice, respectable, quiet people. You're to be particularly demure, easy to get along with."

"What do I tell her my name is?"

"*You* don't tell her," I said. "*I* tell her."

"And what do you tell her?"

"That you're Mrs. Lam, of course."

She said, "And I suppose you're going to promise that if

29

we stay in a single apartment you'll be the soul of honor and discretion at all times."

"Don't be silly," I said.

She looked at me with a flush of anger starting to stain her face.

"Therefore," I said, "I won't be there. I'll be away from home. I'm just leaving on a trip. You'll sit there for a few hours and monitor the telephone calls. If anybody asks for Evelyn Ellis pretend to misunderstand them. If you can get by acting the part of Evelyn Ellis you'll do. If you can't you'll be very friendly over the telephone and state that Miss Ellis probably won't be in for some time, but that you'll try to get a message to her. You'll definitely try to find out who's talking but do it in a nice way so it doesn't arouse suspicions. Be friendly and visit with them. If they're men, your voice will be particularly seductive."

"But why in the world should we rent an apartment?" she asked. "Good heavens, Donald, you know what will happen if Bertha finds out and——"

"In this business," I said, "you can't wait for the breaks. You have to make your own breaks and you have to keep moving. Come on."

We entered the Breeze-Mount and rang the bell of the apartment marked MANAGER—MARLENE CHARLOTTE.

The woman who came out in answer to our ring was in the forties. She was a fairly big woman who had started to sag. There was an expressionless placidity about her face which made it seem she felt everything that could possibly happen had already happened.

"Yes?" she asked, looking us over appraisingly.

"I heard that you were expecting a vacancy next month," I said.

"We have three vacancies right now," she said.

"May we look at them?"

"Certainly," she said, and again sized us up, this time more carefully.

Elsie said demurely, "We both work. We'll be here nights and weekends but not during the day."

"No children?" the manager asked.

Elsie shook her head, then the corners of her mouth

twist a bit as though she were about ready to cry. "Not any more," she said. "No children."

"Well, come with me," Mrs. Charlotte said, taking some keys from the board. "I have some apartments I think you'll like."

The first one she showed was neat as a pin and had no telephone. The next one was a larger apartment, with no phone.

Elsie glanced at me surreptitiously and I shook my head.

"Don't you—don't you have anything else?" she asked.

"I have one that's just been vacated," Mrs. Charlotte said. "It hasn't been cleaned up. It's just the way the person left it. She moved out sometime during the night and left me a note."

"May we look at it?" Elsie said, somewhat dubiously.

Mrs. Charlotte led us to the apartment I wanted.

There was a private telephone and the place was in a mess. The tenant who had moved out had made no attempt to disguise the haste of her departure. A wastebasket was crammed to overflowing with the various debris that a person would keep for a while in bureau drawers only to discard when packing up to leave. There were crumpled papers, a pair of old shoes, stockings with runs, and a broken coathanger. More crumpled papers were on the floor of the closet.

Mrs. Charlotte gave an exclamation of annoyance. "The maid was supposed to get in here and clean some of this stuff out," she said.

I looked over at Elsie and raised my eyebrows.

"Well, honey," I asked, "what do you think? Of course it's hard to judge a place in this condition but I have an idea it's just what we want."

Elsie said dubiously, "Yes, I suppose so, but, Donald, you must remember we have to move into a place right away."

"Yes," I said lugubriously, "we do, for a fact. I'll tell you, honey, this place is exactly what we've been looking for. It's only the fact that it isn't clean that——"

Mrs. Charlotte said, "What do you mean when you say you have to move in right away?"

I said, "We've been staying with friends and every time

31

we tried to move they wanted us to remain on with them. They have a small child that they won't trust with a baby-sitter and because we were there they had quite a bit of freedom for the first time in months. Then the man's parents showed up this morning. They'd written they were coming but the letter miscarried. We're going to have to get out right away."

I suddenly whipped a billfold out of my pocket and said, "I'll tell you what. We'll pay the rent now in advance but we'll take off five dollars because of the condition of the apartment. The maid can dump the stuff tomorrow but if you can get some clean linen, we'll move in. Unfortunately I've got to go to San Francisco but Elsie can stay right here. I'll finish bringing our stuff in. Then we can phone our friends that we've found a place. They were terribly concerned. They wanted to have their folks go to a hotel tonight but I told them we'd be sure to find a place."

Mrs. Charlotte hesitated, said, "How long will you be here? Do you want a year's lease?"

I said, "I'd prefer not to take a year's lease unless we have to, because there is a possibility I'll be transferred."

"What sort of work are you in, Mr. Lam?"

"High-security work," I said. "Of course, if you want references I can get you some of the best. However, as long as I'm here you'll have the cash in advance right on the dot."

Her face broke into a sagging smile. "Well, of course I don't like to have you folks move into an apartment looking like this, but ... if Mrs. Lam doesn't mind ..."

"It's quite all right," Elsie said, looking around. "Frankly, however, I won't try to do much cleaning up until after the maid gets in tomorrow."

"That's fine," Mrs. Charlotte said. "I'll have some linen up here right away."

She said to me, "Come downstairs and I'll give you a receipt for the rent."

The phone started to ring.

I frowned and said, "I suppose that's never been dis-connected."

"No, it's still in the name of the other occupant, Evelyn Ellis," she said.

32

"Oh, well, we'll get that straightened out," I said, taking her by the arm and shooting Elsie a significant glance.

I led the manager out of the door and down to the elevator.

Elsie moved over toward the telephone.

Down in the office Mrs. Charlotte gave me a receipt and I told her, "I'll run up and tell the wife I'm going out to pick up our stuff."

I hurried back up to the apartment.

"Find out who it was, Elsie?" I asked.

She said, "Apparently you've been getting around, Donald."

"How come?"

"This," she said, "was a gentleman who inquired for Evelyn Ellis. I told him that she wasn't here but that I expected to be in touch with her and I could give her a message if necessary. He said to have her call Mr. Calhoun, the public relations man. I told him that I didn't think she'd be free to call, that she was going to call me but that was all the telephoning she'd have a chance to do. He wanted to know who I was and I told him I was her roommate, so he finally let down his hair and told me to tell her that a Mr. Lam had been asking questions, that he had become suspicious of Mr. Lam and on a hunch had looked Lam up in the telephone book. There was only one Donald Lam he'd been able to find and he was a member of the firm of Cool & Lam, private investigators. So Mr. Calhoun asked me if I'd be sure to get in touch with Evelyn and tell her a private eye was on her trail.

"I told him I'd try and reach Evelyn right away and asked him if he had any idea what you were after and he said he didn't, that you were posing as a writer but that you certainly were on the track of something. He said you tried to make a circuitous approach, but he'd had you figured out right from the start."

"Interesting," I said.

"Isn't it?"

"Where's the letter that came by messenger?" I asked.

She opened her purse and handed me an envelope. I looked it over, pulled out my knife, cut the envelope along the edge, then pulled out a sheet of note paper. It was covered with masculine handwriting and was signed "Standley Downer." It read:

Dear Mr. Lam:

Hello, Sucker!

I understand Hazel has asked you to get her fifty grand back. For your information, Hazel is all finished. I am the one who gave it to her, so now I'm taking it back. She hasn't a dime left. It serves her right. If you expect her to pay you anything it won't be in cash.

You're a businessman. Don't let her make a sucker out of you the way she tried to make a boob out of me.

I presume she told you she said "yes" in front of an altar. For your information, it was on the back seat of an automobile. She never got me near an altar. Every cent she ever had is money I gave her.

Any story she may have given you about inheriting the money is just so much malarkey. I told her I was giving her this wad of dough. She fell for that line. It was nice while it lasted.

If you feel you can run your business on promises go ahead and be a sucker. The only money she has to eat on is what she borrowed on her equity in the car.

So long, Sucker!

I handed the letter to Elsie. She read it and her eyes widened. "Donald, how did *he* know about all this?" she asked.

I said, "He might have a pipeline in to police headquarters, he might have a newspaper reporter tipping him off, or Hazel may have a friend in whom she's confiding who is double-crossing her."

"Interesting possibilities, aren't they?" she said.

I nodded. "The guy works fast."

"What was his object in writing you?" she asked.

"Trying to get me to lay off the case by telling me there wouldn't be any money for a fee," I said.

"But, Donald, if they're not married, doesn't that leave you in something of a spot? If you find him he'll tell you to go jump in the lake."

I said, "After I find him Hazel is supposed to take over. You remember she said she had something on him?"

Elsie thought things over for a moment, then said, "Donald, do you know what *I* think?"

"What?" I asked.

"That there's collusion between Hazel and Standley. He assisted in stealing the money from the—— Donald, they're going to get *you* involved in this money deal and make *you* some sort of a cat's-paw."

"Could be," I said.

"Donald, it *has* to be! This letter must have been written not too long after Hazel left your office."

"It's possible," I said.

"Donald, don't you understand? They're working hand in glove, trying to trap you in some way."

"If that's true, we can't stop them from being hand and glove," I said.

"But what do we do?" she asked.

"You sit right here, Mrs. Lam," I said. "You make up the bed. You ride hard on that telephone. You answer it every time it rings. You tell them that you're Evelyn's roommate, that Evelyn is going to call you sometime later on and that you'll take any messages."

"How long do I stay here?"

"Until I get back to relieve you," I said. "Ring up the office. Say you had to leave early on account of a headache. Don't let the switchboard operator get Bertha on the line.

"Incidentally, there's an enclosed garage space that goes with this apartment. I'm doing down now and take a look in there. You prowl through the wastebasket and see if there's anything that would give us a clue. I don't think there is, but you can give it a prowl."

I headed for the door.

Elsie stood looking at me dubiously.

"What's the matter?" I asked. "Afraid?"

"Oh, no," she said. "It's just that I'm trying to reconcile my ideas of a honeymoon with you to a dirty wastebasket filled with some other woman's discarded clothing."

"That's the trouble with realization," I said. "It's always short of anticipation. You should think of how I feel."

CHAPTER FOUR

THE garage was padlocked. Mrs. Charlotte reluctantly gave me the key and told me it was the last key she had and be sure not to lose it. The previous occupant had taken the key with her when she left. She'd turned in the key to the apartment but had kept the key to the garage.

I assured Mrs. Charlotte I'd have a duplicate key made at my own expense and give her back her key.

I drove out to the garage, fitted the key to the padlock, snapped back the hasp and opened the door.

The only ventilation was through a little louvred window in the side wall just below the roof. The place was fairly dark and smelled musty.

I turned on the light.

There was a collection öf junk from several previous occupants; an old casing, a jack handle, an ancient hub cap, some empty oil cans, some greasy coveralls, a water-stiffened piece of chamois skin, old and worn, and a brand-new trunk in the middle of the floor.

I examined it carefully. It was of a standard, expensive make and it was securely locked.

I gave the matter thoughtful consideration. The trunk was sitting in the exact center of the floor where anyone entering the garage couldn't help but see it. Evelyn had left Mrs. Charlotte a note stating she was leaving, that her rent was paid up, that Mrs. Charlotte could re-rent the apartment. She had placed the key to the apartment in the note but she hadn't returned the key to the garage.

Quite obviously, then, Evelyn intended to give the key to the garage to some person to come and get the trunk and take it to her, or ship it to her. She had given this person the key to the garage and, so there could be no question, had left the trunk in the middle of the floor where it couldn't possibly be missed.

I left the garage, locked the padlock, jumped in the agency heap and cruised down the street until I came to the first good-looking hardware store I could find.

I bought the very best padlock in the store. It was

guaranteed to be unpickable. There were two keys which came with the padlock.

I hurried back to the garage, unlocked the old padlock, made sure the trunk was still there, put the new padlock on the door, drove down the block and called Mrs. Charlotte.

When I had her on the phone I said, "This is Mr. Lam, Mrs. Charlotte. I'm going to have to store some rather valuable papers in the garage and I don't like the idea of the previous occupant having a key which hasn't been turned in, so I'm going to put a new padlock on the door. I'm having extra keys made for you."

"Why, that's very thoughtful of you, Mr. Lam," she said. "I have a call in for the maid. I'm trying to get the apartment cleaned up before evening."

"Don't worry too much about it," I said. "My wife will get the worst of it out of the way. I'll be seeing you later."

"You'll be in this evening?"

"I'll probably have to go to San Francisco," I said. "I'm waiting on a call now, but I'll let you know. My wife will be there."

I stopped in at a baggage store, bought myself a trunk of the same make and size as the one in the garage, went to my apartment and packed it full of clothes.

I wrote myself a letter addressing myself as George Biggs Gridley. The letter read:

Dear Mr. Gridley:

I am sorry we didn't get together in Las Vegas. I couldn't join you in Los Angeles, but I expect to get in touch with you while you're at the Golden Gateway Hotel in San Francisco.

Once we get together I think an equitable division of the property can be worked out.

I signed the letter with the initials "L. N. M." and placed it in the side pocket of a sports coat I packed in the trunk.

After I'd closed the trunk, I packed a suitcase and a handbag, taking everything I'd need to keep me going for a week. Then I drove back to the Breeze-Mount Apartments and lugged the suitcase and handbag into the elevator.

Elsie had gone through the wastebasket and had a few crumpled papers smoothed out on the desk.

"Find anything?" I asked.

"There are some telephone numbers on these pieces of paper," she said. "One of them, I think, is a San Francisco number."

"That's fine," I said.

I copied the numbers into my notebook. "Anything else?"

"Rancid cosmetics, ends of lipsticks, various and sundry articles of female litter," she said, "and that's about it."

"Okay," I said. "The landlady's trying to get hold of the maid so you can have the place cleaned up. Call a taxicab. When the cab comes, go to your apartment, pack up a suitcase with whatever you'll need for two days and hurry back."

She started to say something, then changed her mind, went to the closet and put on her coat.

"Give me the key," I said. "You can close the door when you go out."

"What will I do when I come back?"

"If I'm not here the key will be at the desk," I told her.

I hurried down to the car, drove it into the driveway, unlocked the new padlock on the garage and took the trunk which was in the center of the floor and moved it far back into the shadows. Then I backed my car halfway into the garage, opened the back, rustled out my trunk and left it right in the middle of the floor where the other trunk had been. Then I drove the car out of the garage, locked the garage with the new padlock, parked my car near the curb and went back up to the apartment.

"Okay, Elsie," I said, "you can leave as soon as the cab comes."

"I'll have to stop by a supermarket and grab some groceries," she said.

"Sure thing," I told her. "Get some coffee, cream, sugar, eggs, salt, bread, bacon—stuff of that sort—and get the place provisioned up. The manager may start checking. Get the taxi driver to carry your stuff to the elevator. If I'm here I'll come and carry it in the rest of the way. Otherwise, you'll have to rustle it in by yourself."

"If you're not here, will you get in touch with me and let me know where you are?"

I took down the number of the telephone and said, "Sure. I'll be in touch with you. Now, you go ahead and get your stuff."

The manager phoned to say the cab had arrived.

"Well," Elsie said, putting on her coat, "as a dutiful wife, I'll follow instructions. I hadn't imagined being married to you could be like this, Donald. I'll be back as fast as I can make it."

After Elsie had left I sat there hoping the phone wouldn't ring. I knew that if it did ring I'd have to let it ring. If a man's voice answered, it would frighten away the quarry. On the other hand, if no one answered the phone, the call would be repeated later. But the manager of the apartment knew I was in. According to my plans she had to know I was there.

I pulled up a chair by the window, propped my feet on another chair and went over the sequence of events in my mind.

The telephone started to ring. I let it ring. It seemed an interminable time before the bell ceased making noise.

I got up and began pacing the floor, impatient with myself for letting Elsie go, yet realizing there was nothing else I could have done under the circumstances.

After fifteen or twenty minutes the telephone rang again and this time it continued to ring and ring and ring. I finally walked over, picked up the phone and said, "What number are you calling, please?"

"For heaven sakes, where have *you* been?" Mrs. Charlotte said. "I *knew* you were up there. I——"

"I couldn't come to the phone right away," I said. "What's the trouble?"

"A man is here who wants to get into the garage," she said. "He is instructed to pick up a trunk."

"He got a letter to that effect?" I asked.

"He has the key to the garage; that is, the key to the old lock. Evelyn Ellis gave it to him. He tried to get in and found that the lock had been changed. You told me you were *going* to change it but you didn't tell me you *had* changed it. I don't have a key."

I said, "I'll be right down and let him in. I'm sorry."

"I can come up and get the key. I just wanted to be sure——"

"No," I said, "I'll come down and open it for him. What does he want to take out?"

"It seems that Miss Ellis, the former tenant, left a trunk there and she sent him to pick up the trunk. That's all he wants."

"Oh, well," I said, "if that's the case, come up in the elevator and I'll give you your key and then *you* can let him in."

I walked down to the elevator and waited until Mrs. Charlotte came up.

"I'm sorry," I said. "I should have left you the key when I changed the padlocks."

"You should have," she snapped. "This is rather inconvenient all around."

"I'm sorry."

I handed her the key to the padlock.

She went down in the elevator.

I hurried down the stairs and stood where I could see the desk.

The man who was standing, talking with her, was the man whose photograph Hazel Downer had given me. He seemed exceedingly nervous.

Mrs. Charlotte walked out to the garage with him to unlock the padlock.

I slipped into the lobby, tossed the key to the apartment on her desk, then sprinted out to the agency car, started the motor and waited.

Mrs. Charlotte escorted the guy across to the garage and opened the door. He thanked her, stepped inside, looked around, walked back to the street, got into a big sedan and backed the sedan in the driveway until the rear of the car was just inside the garage. Then he got out and opened the trunk of the car and put my trunk, which I had left standing invitingly in the center of the floor, into the car. The lid of the car trunk wouldn't go all the way down but he tied it with rope so it wouldn't fly up. Then he drove out of the driveway and I swung in behind him long enough to get a good look at his license number. It was NYB 241.

After that, I dropped quite a ways behind and didn't crowd him until we got into traffic heavy enough so that he wouldn't notice I was following.

He drove to the Union Depot, parked the car long enough to get a porter to unload the trunk, then drove on to a parking space. I parked my car, drove back and saw him buy a ticket on the Lark to San Francisco. He came out, picked up the porter, went to the baggage room and checked the trunk.

I drove back to the apartment house, opened the garage padlock with my key, backed the agency car in and picked up the trunk I had moved back into the dark corner of the garage. I made time down to the Union Station, bought a ticket on the Lark to San Francisco and checked the trunk. Then I parked my car in the depot garage and called the apartment.

Elsie answered. Her voice sounded thin and a little frightened.

"What's new?" I asked.

"Oh, Donald," she said. "I'm so glad you called. I'm scared."

"What's wrong?"

"Some man called. He didn't ask who I was or anything. He simply said, 'Tell Standley he has until tomorrow morning to get me that ten grand. Otherwise, it's just too bad.'"

"I tried to ask who was talking but the party at the other end of the line just hung up."

I said, "Now look, Elsie, don't get frightened. You're all right. Sit tight. Answer the telephone. Don't tell anybody that you're Evelyn Ellis. Simply say that you will try to get a message to Miss Ellis. If anyone starts pinning you down, tell them that you are the party that moved into the apartment after Evelyn Ellis moved out, but that you have reason to believe she's coming back to pick up messages. If they ask what your name is, act as if they're trying to flirt and tell them that that isn't important. Don't tell anyone any more than you're a *friend* of Evelyn Ellis or that you know her. Get what information you can, but if it comes to a showdown, simply say that you're the new tenant. And if anybody gets rough, tell them that they'd better talk with Mrs. Charlotte, the manager."

"Donald, are you coming back out here?" she asked.

"I'm sorry," I told her. "I'm going to be out for a while."

"How long?"

"All night."

"Donald!"

"Did you want me there ... all night?"

"No ... I'm ... I don't want to be alone."

"All married people have to make adjustments," I said.

"This is one hell of a honeymoon," she said and hung up.

I went to a drugstore, bought a light nylon handbag, bought shaving things, toothbrush and a few toilet articles, then went out to Olvera Street and had a nice Mexican dinner. After that, I strolled down to the Union Depot, got aboard the Lark, took care not to go through either the club car or the diner to avoid being seen, entered my bedroom, closed the door and went to sleep.

I didn't go in for breakfast because I didn't want to be trapped in the dining car. When the train got into San Francisco I tried to make myself as inconspicuous as possible. I carried my own light overnight bag and didn't go near the baggage wagons where the red-cap porters distribute the baggage.

I grabbed a cab, went to the Golden Gateway Hotel and registered under my own name, then told the clerk, "I expect to be joined by George Biggs Gridley. He isn't here yet, but I want him near me. I'll register him in and pay for the adjoining room. You can give me the key and I'll turn it over to Gridley when he comes in. I'll pay for the first day in cash. Later on, if we stay more than one day, we can make credit arrangements."

I took out my billfold.

The clerk was all smiles.

He gave me two adjoining rooms.

I looked up a drive-yourself car agency, rented a station wagon, drove back down to Third and Townsend, turned in my baggage check and got the trunk.

It was a reasonably heavy trunk and there was something about the balance that bothered me. It seemed to have the weight all in the bottom.

I drove up to the hotel, unloaded the car, drove into a

parking place, came back and had the trunk taken to the room I'd rented under the name of George Biggs Gridley. I thought that was a nice name.

I called the bell captain, said, "I'm in a hell of a jam. I've lost the key to my trunk. I've got to get it open."

He said, "The porter keeps a whole bunch of keys. He can probably handle it. I'll send him up."

I waited about five minutes and the porter came in with a key ring that looked as though it had a hundred keys on it of assorted shapes and sizes.

It took the porter less than thirty seconds to find a key that clicked back the lock on the trunk.

He took the two dollars I handed him and grinned. "It's a cinch," he said. "These locks depend mostly on the shape of the key. They don't put anything very elaborate in them in the way of tumblers. It's just a question of finding something that fits."

When he had left I opened the trunk.

It was filled to the brim with woolen blankets. In the bottom of the trunk, wedged in by blankets so they wouldn't jiggle around, were some cards and books that were full of cabalistic figures.

I sat on the floor and studied the cards and the books. I couldn't make heads or tails of them. All I knew for sure was that they dealt in large sums of money, but there were no names, no words of any sort; just combinations of figures. Over in the right-hand column there would be figures: 20—50—1C—2C—5C—7C—2G—1G—.

Apparently the C's represented hundreds and the G's thousands—that much I felt I could use as a starter.

Then there were cards. These cards each contained a number at the top and a series of notations.

I selected one at random. It read 0051 364. Below these numbers was 4—5—59—10—1; 8—5—59—4—1+.

I studied several of the cards. The number at the top quite frequently ended 364. The numbers on the lower part of the cards were always separated by minus signs but the end would sometimes be plus, sometimes minus.

I pulled everything out of the trunk and started looking it over.

It was quite a while before I found the false-bottom

compartment. I wouldn't have found it then if I hadn't turned the thing up and tapped around with my knuckles.

A movable board was held in place by concealed screws. This board slid out after I had removed those small screws, so carefully concealed that it was almost impossible to find them. The heads had been covered with cloth of exactly the same pattern as the lining of the trunk.

The compartment below was filled with thousand-dollar bills.

I counted them. There were exactly fifty-two one-thousand-dollar bills. I counted twice to make sure, then I took out fifty of the bills, carefully replaced the remaining two in the secret compartment, slid the board back into place and replaced the screws.

Then I carefully replaced the blankets in the trunk. I ran a handkerchief over the things I had touched to be sure I left no fingerprints on the inside of the trunk.

I went down to the cashier's office. "I'm Mr. Lam," I said. "I have to check out. My bill is paid."

She looked it up, said, "But you checked in only a short time ago, Mr. Lam."

"I know. I'm sorry. I had to change my plans."

She frowned. "Did you wish a refund?"

"Heavens, no. I've used the room. That's all right. I just wanted to have the records straight."

She gave me a receipt and a smile.

"All right. You're checked out. I'm sorry you couldn't stay longer."

"So am I. I'll be back, however."

I walked over to the mail desk.

"A message for George Biggs Gridley?" I asked, showing the key to Gridley's room.

"No messages, Mr. Gridley."

I frowned. "Please check again."

She did. There were no messages. That bothered me a lot. By right Gridley's phone should have been hot by this time.

I went back to the trunk, took out the books and cards, put them in a heavy pasteboard carton, sent them by express to myself in Los Angeles, then drove to the Happy Daze Camera Company.

I went inside. It was run by a Japanese. He came to meet me, bowing and scraping.

"I want to see a good used camera," I said. "And I want a box of double-weight five by seven enlarging paper."

He got the paper first.

I opened the box of paper while he was getting out the camera to show me. I slipped out about fifteen sheets of photographic paper, kicked these sheets under the counter and slipped the fifty one-thousand-dollar bills in where the photographic paper had been.

The man who was waiting on me was evidently the manager of the place. There was another Japanese who was older and who had been watching me curiously, but an attractive woman came in and occupied his attention up at the new camera counter at the front end of the store.

I noticed her out of the corner of my eye but kept my attention on the manager, who was scurrying around trying to clinch the sale.

I picked out one of the cameras he brought over. "How about a case for this?" I asked.

He bowed and smiled and scurried away again.

I made sure that the fifty thousand dollars in bills fitted snugly into the package of enlarging paper and put the black paper wrappings back around the paper, the cover back on the box.

When the manager came back with the case for the camera I haggled for a few minutes about price, then said, "All right, I'll take it. Now then, I want all this shipped at once."

"Shipped?"

"Shipped."

"Where to, please?"

I gave him one of my cards. "I want this sent to my personal attention at Los Angeles and I want it sent *at once* by air express. I want someone to get in a cab and personally take it to the air-express office. Mark the package 'Rush and Special Handling.'"

I pulled out a wallet and started counting out money.

"Yes, yes," he said. "Very good. Right away."

"You'll send a special messenger down to the airport?"

"Right away," he promised. "I call a cab, right away."

"Pack it up nicely," I said, "in excelsior so it won't be damaged in transit."

"Oh, yes. Yes, of course."

"I mean immediately, right now. I want that camera in Los Angeles by evening. It has to be sent down with special handling charges. You understand?"

"Will do. Very good."

He called out something in Japanese to the man at the other end of the store who was waiting on the woman.

That man answered him without looking around.

I looked over at the counter. The young woman had her back turned toward me and was inspecting a camera. The Japanese assistant seemed annoyed that he was being interrupted in making a sale.

"All right," I said. "You get it down there. Remember now, it's important."

I took the receipt which he gave me and walked out.

The woman was still looking at cameras. I tried to get a glimpse of her face but she wasn't interested enough in me to even look up from the camera she was inspecting. She sure had a figure—from the back.

I went to a phone booth and called Elsie at the apartment.

"Hi, gorgeous!" I said. "How was the first night of the honeymoon?"

"Donald," she said, "I won't stay here unless you stay with me. I'm so frightened. I——"

"What happened?"

"Twice during the night the phone rang," she said. "I picked up the receiver and before I could say hello a man's voice said, 'Tell Standley he has until ten o'clock tomorrow morning,' and then before I could say anything the party hung up both times."

I said, "All right, Elsie. Tell Mrs. Charlotte that I've been called to New York and want you to join me. Tell her she can have the perishable provisions. Call a cab. Load in your baggage and go to the office. Say you've been sick. Avoid talking with Bertha."

"Oh Donald! I was hoping you'd get back here—I didn't sleep a wink. . . . Tell me, are you all right?"

"Sure," I said. "I'm sitting pretty. Now listen, Elsie, at noon a certain party is going to call up—Abigail Smythe—and remember the *y* and the *e*."

"Yes," she said. "What do I do about that?"

"Now, this," I told her, "is going to be tricky. You tell her to go to the airport in her car and be there at three o'clock this afternoon. Tell her to try to see that she isn't followed, if possible.

"Tell her I'm arriving at three ten on United Air Lines. Tell her to find out if my flight is on time, bring her car up and put it in the three-minute parking zone. Tell her to unlock the trunk and raise the lid as though she had gone to get some baggage. That will give her all the time we'll need. At precisely three twenty-five I'll get a cab. I'll give the cab driver the address but will fumble around with my notebook before I get the address for him. That will give her time to see just what cab I am taking. Tell her to follow the cab.

"No matter where the cab goes or what it does, she's to follow the cab. She doesn't need to be subtle about it. Just follow the cab. That's all she needs to know and all she needs to do.

"You got that?"

"I've got it," she said.

"Good girl," I told her, and hung up.

I drove to the airport, turned in my rented car, caught the Los Angeles plane and disembarked right on time.

At three twenty-five I walked out to the sidewalk by the corner of the sun deck in front of the upstairs restaurant, looked around as though trying to orient myself, then went across to a taxicab, got inside and fumbled around with a notebook, pretending to look for an address.

After a moment the cab driver said, "Well, I'll start and you can find the address while we're moving."

"It's okay," I said, "I know the general neighbourhood, but I can't recall the street and number. You'll have to just follow instructions. I'll tell you where to go."

"Good enough," he said.

The cab swung out into traffic and I settled back against the cushions. I didn't look behind until after we had got out on the boulevard where there was some relatively open country. Then I saw a crossroad ahead and said to the cab driver, "Turn off to the right on this road."

"This next one?"

"That's the one."

The cab driver said, "Okay," pulled over to the right-hand lane of traffic and made a turn.

It wasn't until after we had made the turn that I looked around.

Hazel Downer, in a sleek-looking sports job, was right behind us.

I had the cab driver drive along until I was certain no one else was following, then I said, "This isn't the street after all. Turn around. We'll have to go back. I guess it's the next one."

The cab driver made a U-turn.

Hazel made a U-turn right behind us. The cab driver said, "Hey, buddy, do you know you're wearing a tail?"

"How come?" I asked.

"I don't know. She's been behind us ever since we left the airport."

"Pull in to the curb," I said. "I'll take a look."

"No rough stuff," the cabbie warned.

"Sure," I said. "Just find out how come, that's all."

The cab pulled in and stopped.

I walked back to Hazel, said, "Anybody been following you?"

"Not that I know of."

"Okay," I said. "Wait here."

I walked back to the cab and said, "That's a coincidence! I didn't recognize her. That's a friend of the woman I was going to meet. She came down to the airport, saw that I didn't recognize her and was about half-mad. She was going to let me run up a cab bill before she blew the horn and took me off the hook. How much is the meter?"

"Two ten," he said.

I gave him five dollars and said, "Okay, buddy, thanks a lot."

He looked at me and grinned. "I *was* going to tell you, you weren't fooling me a damned bit; but now I'm going to tell you, you don't even have to try."

He drove off.

I took my light handbag, walked back to Hazel's car and said, "Okay. Wait until the cab gets well ahead, then make another U-turn and go back out this street."

I got in beside her.

It was one of those low jobs with a surprising amount of leg room and Hazel was showing lots of nylon. She had wonderful gams.

She made a token motion of pulling her skirt down, laughed nervously and said, "It's no use, Donald. I just can't drive this damned car without giving an exhibition."

"Suits me," I said.

"I thought it would," she said. "Is the cab far enough ahead now?"

"No. Let him get out of sight in traffic so he won't know that we made another turn. He'll think we're following along behind him—just in case anyone should ask him."

"My, but you're suspicious!"

"Sometimes it pays," I told her. "All right. Make another U-turn now and go back to the east."

She swung the car. "Do you know where this road goes?"

"Comes out around Inglewood someplace," I said. "Just keep going."

We followed the road, finally came to a place where there were some houses, then more houses, then a crossroad, then more houses. I said, "Start hitting the crossroads. I'll watch the road behind us.

"Can we go someplace where we can talk?" I asked after another few minutes.

"To my apartment," she said.

"Don't be silly," I told her. "They're watching your apartment like hawks."

"Donald, I don't think they are."

"Why?"

"Because I've been coming and going and there hasn't been anyone around. I've driven the car places several times and each time have made absolutely certain that no one was following."

"How did you do that?"

"The same way you did. I'd get in the car and drive out

on a lot of side roads where I could spot any traffic coming behind."

"You sure you didn't ditch a shadow by going through a traffic signal just as it was changing or something?"

"No, Donald. I deliberately tried to make myself a sitting duck in case anyone was following."

"Just the same," I said, "we're not going to take a chance on your apartment. Where else can we go?"

"What about *your* apartment?"

"They may be watching that, too."

She said, "I have a friend. I can phone her. I think she'd let us use her apartment."

"Okay," I said. "Let's get to a phone."

We swung back onto a boulevard. She stopped at a phone booth, called, came back, said, "It's all right. My friend will leave the door unlocked and she'll give us an hour and a half. That should be all the time we need."

"Should be," I said. "Where is this place?"

"Not too far. We'll be there in ten minutes. She thinks I'm having an affair with a married man and she's dying with curiosity."

I hitched around in the seat and kept looking behind us.

"Well?" she asked.

"Well what?"

"Am I or am I not?"

"What?"

"Having an affair with a married man?"

"How would I know?"

"Oh, all right, I'll come right out with it. Donald, are you married?"

"No. Why?"

"Nothing."

"But you are," I said.

She started to say something, then checked herself.

We got to her friend's apartment house, parked the car and took the elevator to the fourth floor. Hazel Downer walked unerringly down to the apartment and opened the door.

There was a long-legged grace about her that made it a pleasure to watch her move.

It was a nice apartment, one that really cost money.

I waited for Hazel to seat herself.

She chose the davenport, so I went over to sit beside her. "All right," I told her, "now let's get to the real truth."

"About what?"

"About the money."

"But I gave you the real truth about the money."

"Don't be silly," I said. "I want to know the *real* truth. I'm not going to lead with my chin."

"But we went all through this yesterday."

"No, we didn't," I said. "You gave me a run-around yesterday about an uncle and all that. Now I want the real low-down."

"Why, Donald? Do you know where the money is?"

"I think I can get it for you."

She leaned forward, her eyes starry, her lips half parted. "All of it?"

"Fifty thousand."

"Donald," she said, "I ... Donald, you're wonderful! You're terrific!"

She looked up at me, holding her chin up, wanting to be kissed. I kept my eyes on the window and just sat there, waiting.

"Donald," she sighed, "you *do* things to me."

"*That's* fine," I told her. "Right now you're stalling for time so you can think up a good story. Evidently this is the only stalling technique you know. I certainly thought you would have taken advantage of the time since yesterday to have thought up a dilly."

"I have," she said, and laughed.

"All right, let's hear it."

"Standley gave me this money."

"For what?"

"Do I have to draw you a diagram?"

"For fifty thousand bucks you do."

"Standley is a gambler, big-time stuff. He always felt he might be wiped out or held up—or even rubbed out."

"Go on."

"He kept some money in the bank, but he wanted to have money where he could get at it at any hour of day or night —in cash."

"And so?"

"So from time to time he'd give me thousand-dollar

bills. He said they were mine. In that way if he went broke no one could claim this money was his, but I could stake him—if I wanted to."

"Phooey," I said, "they'd simply claim the money was his and that——"

"No, Donald, whenever he'd give me these bills he'd take my manicure scissors and cut off just the very smallest piece on the corner ... and finally I got fifty of these bills ... and then he ran out on me ... and I suppose this latest paramour of his is holding the stake."

"But he gave you title to the money, so the——"

Heavy knuckles sounded on the door.

"Better see who that is," I said.

She made a gesture of annoyance. "It's some tradesman or somebody who wants to see my friend. Just a minute."

She jumped to her feet, switched her skirt into place, walked over to the door with her characteristic long-legged grace, opened it and was pushed back almost off her feet as Frank Sellers shoved his way into the room and slammed the door behind him.

"Hello, Pint Size," Sellers said to me.

"Well, I *like* this!" Hazel Downer said angrily. "You have your nerve barging in like this. You——"

Sellers said, "Now then, let's cut out the monkey business, you two."

"I don't care to have you talk to me that way," Hazel Downer said. "You——"

I interrupted. "Look, Hazel, do you know a good lawyer?"

"Why, yes," she said.

"Telephone him and tell him to come over here fast," I said.

Sellers said, "That isn't going to do either one of you any good. I warned you about this, Donald. I'm going to bust you wide open—and I'm not going to administer an anesthetic while I perform the operation either."

"Get that lawyer on the phone," I said to Hazel Downer, "and start working fast."

Sellers sat down in a chair, crossed his legs, pulled a cigar out of his pocket, bit off the end and spit it into an ash tray. He scraped a match into flame.

Hazel moved toward the telephone. Sellers made a grab at her, circled her with his arm.

"She's calling a lawyer," I said. "A citizen has that right. Try stopping her and see what it gets you."

"Take your hand off my body," Hazel said.

Sellers hesitated, then took his arm away. "All right, go ahead and call your lawyer. Then I'm going to show you both something."

Sellers lit his cigar. Hazel made a low-voiced phone call and hung up. Sellers took the cigar out of his mouth, looked Hazel Downer over as she returned to the davenport.

"Well, Bright Eyes," he said, "you really got yourself in a mess now."

"Do you have a charge against me?" she asked.

"So far," Sellers said, "receiving stolen property and criminal conspiracy. I think we can go a step farther and convict you of being an accessory after the fact, attempted extortion, and perhaps a few other things."

Sellers turned to me. His eyes were burning with suppressed rage. "*You* double-crossing bastard!"

"What do you mean, double-crossing?"

"I warned you to leave this one alone," he said.

"You warned me," I said. "You aren't the legislature. You aren't passing the laws. I didn't double-cross you. I didn't promise you I'd lay off. I'm running a legitimate business."

"Says you!"

"Say I," I said.

Sellers said, "Well, if you folks are finished with the phone I'll put through a call myself, just to let Headquarters know where I am."

He went over to the phone, dialed the number of Headquarters, said, "This is Sergeant Sellers. I'm at——" He drew back to look at the number on the telephone, "Hightower 7-74103. It's an apartment but I don't know who rents it yet. I'm with Hazel Downer and Donald Lam. I think we're going to button up the rest of that armored truck case. If you want me, get me here."

Sellers hung up the phone, came over to where I was sitting on the davenport and stood looming above me, looking down at me ominously.

53

"I hate to do it on account of Bertha," he said. "Bertha is a good gal; greedy but square—and she plays fair with the police.

"You're a two-timing chisler. You always have been. You play both ends against the middle. So far you've always come out smelling like a rose. This time it's going to be different."

I looked past him to Hazel. "Did you get him?"

"Yes."

"Is he coming over?"

"Yes."

"Is he good?"

"The best."

"How long will it take him to get here?"

"He's coming right away."

"How long?"

"Ten minutes. He's right here in this neighbourhood."

"Do something for me," I said. "Don't say a word until your lawyer gets here. Don't answer any questions. Don't even say yes or no."

Sellers said. "That won't help her, Lam. You don't know what I know."

"What *do* you know?" I asked.

Sellers took a notebook out of his pocket, said, "Hazel Clune, alias Hazel Downer. Living in open and notorious cohabitation with Standley Downer. Standley has a record."

"A record!" Hazel exclaimed.

"Don't be so coy," Sellers said. "He's a con man and a promoter. He's served time in two Federal prisons. He's out on parole at the present time and we can violate him any time we want.

"So far I can't prove that Standley was a pal of Herbert Baxley, but they were in Leavenworth at the same time, so they know each other all right. So Standley and Herbert Baxley got together and figured out a scheme for lifting a hundred grand out of this armored truck. After they got the money they split it two ways and——"

The phone started ringing.

Sellers frowned at it a moment, then said, "I'll just answer that and save you the trouble. This may be for me."

He went over to the telephone, picked it up, said cautiously, "Hello," then settled himself and said, "Yeah, talking—go ahead."

For almost a minute a voice made sounds in the receiver. Sellers frowned, at first incredulously, then reached up with his right hand and took the cigar out of his mouth as though that would help him hear better. He said, "You're sure? Give me that again."

Sellers put the cigar on the telephone stand, pulled a notebook from his pocket and made notes. "Once more," he said. "I want to get those names.

"Okay," he said, "I've got Downer and Lam right here. I'll bring them in. Hold everything until I get there. Don't notify the press for a while. I want to sit on this myself."

He hung up the telephone, then suddenly, with a quick motion of his hand, jerked out his revolver and pointed it at me. "Up," he said.

There was something in his eyes that I had never seen before.

I got up.

"Turn around."

I turned around.

"Walk over to the wall."

I walked over to the wall.

"Face the wall, stand back three feet, spread your feet apart, then lean forward and put your palms against the wall."

I did as he ordered.

Sellers said to Hazel Downer, "Get over there against the wall."

"I won't do any such thing," she said.

"Okay," Sellers said. "You're a woman. I can't frisk you, but I'm warning you, this is business. Either one of you make a false move and you're going to stop lead."

He walked over to the davenport.

I tried to see what was going on but my arms were up so that I could only get a flurry of motion. I saw skirts kicking up, an expanse of leg, a high-heeled shoe kicking, heard a metallic click and a woman's scream and then Hazel Downer said, "Why, you—you beast! You've handcuffed me!"

"You're damn right I've handcuffed you," Sellers said.

"Make another try with those spike heels and I'll sap you over the head. I may not be able to search you, but I can sure as hell draw your fangs."

He walked over to me, shoved one foot up against my leg. His hands started running over me in a swift search.

"Keep your hands against the wall, Lam," he said. "Don't move. If you do, you're going to get hurt."

His hands went over me, searching every inch of my clothes.

"All right," he said, "you're clean. Now, stand back there and take the things out of your pocket. Put them on that table."

I did as I was told.

"Everything," Sellers said. "Money, keys, everything."

I put everything on the table.

"Turn your pockets inside out."

I followed his instructions.

Knuckles sounded on the door.

Sellers jumped back until he was against the wall. He turned his gun on the door. "Come in," he called.

The door opened. A man in the late thirties, smiling affably, entered the room, then jerked to a standstill as he saw Frank Sellers' gun pointed at him, saw me standing there with my pockets wrongside out and Hazel Downer sitting on the davenport, her wrists handcuffed behind her back.

"What the devil!" he exclaimed.

"Police," Frank Sellers said. "Who are you?"

"I'm Madison Ashby," he said, "an attorney at law."

"Her lawyer?" Sellers asked.

"Yes."

"She's sure going to need one," Sellers said. And then, after a moment, added, "Bad."

"Maddy," Hazel said, "will you *please* make this baboon get these things off my wrists and find out what this is all about?"

Sellers made a little gesture with the gun. "Sit down," he said to Ashby. Then he nodded to me. "Sit down, Lam. Keep your hands in sight."

Sellers remained standing, holding the gun.

"May I ask what this is all about?" Ashby inquired.

Sellers ignored his inquiry, turned to me. "So you went to San Francisco, Pint Size," Sellers said. "And you took a trunk."

"That's a crime?" I asked.

"Murder's a crime."

"What are you talking about?"

"Right now," he said, "I'm talking about a man named Standley Downer, who was murdered in the Caltonia Hotel in San Francisco. Your trunk was standing open in the middle of the floor and the clothing and stuff that was in the trunk were scattered to hell and gone all over the room."

Sellers read the startled surprise in my eyes.

"Go on," he said, "put on an act. You're a smart little pint-sized bastard, and a hell of a good actor. You did a swell job of that. You——"

He stopped as Hazel's scream, sounding shrill and hysterical, knifed through the room.

Sellers turned to her. "Well, now," he said, "*that's* a nice performance. You pulled just the right timing on that, just the right delay to think what to do, just the right timing to save Donald here from having to answer questions and giving him a minute to think.

"Now then, sister, I've got news for *you! You* were in San Francisco last night, too. You were calling on a babe named Evelyn Ellis at this same Caltonia Hotel. This gal was registered in the Caltonia under the name of Beverly Kettle. She was in Room 751. You told her you didn't give a damn about Standley Downer, that she could have him for keeps, but that you wanted what he'd taken from you and if you didn't get it there'd be lots of trouble.

"You called her several naughty words and she——"

Hazel started to interrupt him to say something.

"Shut up," Madison Ashby snapped at her.

Sellers turned to look at him with sober eyes. "I *could* kick *you* the hell out of here," he said.

"You could," Ashby said, "and just on the chance that you might want to do it, I'm going to advise my client what to do. Say nothing, Hazel. Absolutely nothing. Don't even give him the time of day. Don't admit anything, don't deny anything, just say nothing except that you won't talk until you have had a chance to confer with your lawyer in private.

"And now," he said, turning to Frank Sellers with a little bow, "since you seem to be concerned about my being here, I'll be on my way."

"The hell you *will*," Sellers said. "You're just a little too eager, my lad. You're anxious to get out and get on the telephone and tip somebody off to something. You're going to stay right here."

"Got a warrant?" Ashby asked.

Sellers backed up, pushed him to one side, walked over to the door, turned the bolt. "I've got something that beats that," he said.

"This is violating my legal rights," Ashby said.

"I'll let you go after a while," Sellers said. "Right now I'm holding you as a material witness."

"A material witness to what?"

"To the fact that Hazel here screamed when I was trying to get an answer out of Donald Lam."

"That wasn't why she screamed," Ashby said. "For your information, Standley Downer is her husband. A woman has a right to scream when she's just learned that her husband has met a violent death and she is left a widow."

Sellers said, "Husband, my eye! For *your* information, this babe is Hazel Clune. She's been going by the name of Downer since she and Standley Downer teamed up.

"For your further information, this Hazel Clune, or Hazel Downer, as she's calling herself, is mixed up to her eyebrows in the robbery of an armored truck. She's been playing around with a crook named Herbert Baxley. She's sore because Standley skipped out with fifty grand from the armored truck job. I guess that she regarded it as community property."

Hazel took a quick breath, again started to say something.

"Shut up," Madison Ashby said. "You say a word to anyone before I've talked with you and I won't touch your case with a ten-foot pole."

Sellers grinned. "Which case?" he asked.

"A case against you for locking her in a room, for falsely accusing her of crime, for defamation of character and slander, so far. I don't know what will come up later on."

Sellers looked at him moodily and said, "You know, I could develop quite a dislike for you."

"Dislike me all you want to," Ashby said. "I'm protecting my client."

Sellers swung back to me. "How the hell did Standley Downer get hold of your trunk?"

Ashby caught my eye, shook his head.

"How would I know?" I asked.

Sellers worried his cigar for a minute, then holstered his gun, walked over to the telephone, dialed a number and said, "Let me talk with Bertha Cool."

He held on to the phone for a moment, then said, "Hello, Bertha. Frank Sellers ... Your partner double-crossed you and double-crossed me."

I could hear Bertha's voice making raucous sounds on the telephone.

"You'd better get over here," Sellers said. "I want to talk with you."

Bertha's voice was a scream which poured sound out of the telephone and made her words audible all over the room. "Where's here?"

Sellers gave her the address. "Now, look," he said, "your boy, Donald, has been cutting corners. I don't know how much damage he's done. He's been to San Francisco. I don't think he killed a guy up there, but the San Francisco police think he did. What's more, he picked up some loot. On that I'll ride along with anybody. You'd better get over here."

Sellers hung up the phone, sat down and watched me speculatively as though trying to read my mind.

I looked at him with a poker face.

"Wouldn't it be funny," Sellers said, "if this guy Standley Downer had the fifty grand from that armored car job with him? Wouldn't it be just too funny for words if he'd put it in a trunk someplace, left his lady-love here flat on her beautiful fanny and took off for San Francisco?"

There was silence in the room.

"And wouldn't it be funny," Sellers went on, "if you got real, real smart, found out what was going on, and decided to cut yourself a piece of cake? You *could* have juggled trunks on the guy. You're a fast worker."

Hazel turned wide startled eyes in my direction.

"Now, the question is," Sellers went on. "how the hell this Standley guy got your trunk if you didn't get his, and if you got his where is it now?

"Now, I'm going to tell you something, Pint Size. You've been up to San Francisco. You came back on the plane and this babe came down to the airport just to meet you. You instructed her to keep running around in her car to see if she was being tailed."

"You can prove that?" I asked.

Sellers rolled the cigar from one end of his mouth to the other, then reached up with his left hand, removed the cigar from his mouth and laughed, a harsh, bitter laugh. "You damned amateurs," he said. "You don't keep up with what's going on."

Sellers walked over to the window, looked down and then motioned to me to come to the window.

"Take a look," he said.

I followed the direction of his finger.

A car in the parking lot had a bright orange cross painted on the top of it.

"Ever hear of a helicopter?" Sellers said. "We've had this babe under observation. I can tell you every move she made. We followed her from the air and when we wanted to do some close work we came down close with the helicopter. Most of the time we could use binoculars and get all the information we wanted.

"When she headed for town yesterday we had a helicopter covering her all the way. She did a lot of zigzagging so as to lose any shadows. Then she beat it to the airport and caught a Western jet for San Francisco. Then she went to call on Evelyn Ellis.

"After she'd cussed Evelyn out, she went down and stuck around in the lobby for a while, apparently waiting for Standley to walk in.

"She sat there for two hours. The clerk didn't want her hanging around the lobby. He knew she was carrying a hatchet for someone. Finally she went to the desk and tried to get a room for the night. The clerk told her he was full up. She hung around a little while longer and then the clerk told her that unescorted women were not permitted in the lobby after ten o'clock at night.

"That's where the San Francisco police let us down. They let her give them the slip.

"The next time we picked her up was when she took an early-morning plane for Los Angeles. We picked up her car at the airport. She made a lot of fancy maneuvers to make certain she wasn't being followed, then hightailed it to her apartment. She was there until shortly before your plane came in, then she drove out to the airport to meet you.

"Now then, Miss Clune or Mrs. Downer, or whatever you want to call yourself, I don't want to jump at conclusions. I'm just telling you that Standley Downer was murdered in San Francisco and I'm asking you where you spent the night."

Hazel said, "If I thought——" Abruptly she caught herself. "No comment," she said. "I do not intend to make any statement until I have had an opportunity to talk with my attorney in private."

"Now, that's a great way for an innocent woman to do," Sellers said. "You want us to think you didn't have anything to do with any murder and yet you won't even tell us where you were last night until after you've talked with an attorney. Is that going to look good in the papers?"

"You tend to your own business in this case," Ashby said, "and we'll attend to ours. We're not trying any case in the newspapers. We'll try it in court."

Abruptly Sellers whirled back to me, started to say something, then got another idea, walked over to the telephone, dialed a number and held the receiver so close to his lips that we couldn't hear what he was saying. He was talking in a low voice which came to us as a rumble of sound but no more.

Sellers said after a moment, "Okay, I'll hold the line. You find out."

Sellers waited with the telephone at his ear, the fingers of his right hand drumming on the telephone table, as he sat in frowning contemplation minute after minute.

The silence in the room could have been cut with a knife. Abruptly the telephone started making little rasping noises. Sellers held the receiver close to his ear as he listened, then began mouthing the cigar.

After a moment he took the cigar out of his mouth, said, "All right," and hung up the telephone.

There was an expression of shrewd satisfaction on his face.

Another two or three minutes passed.

Sellers went back to the phone and made another call in a low voice, said, "Okay, call me back."

He hung up and sat in the chair for two or three minutes until the phone rang, then picked it up, said, "Hello . . . no, she isn't. However, I'll take a message for you. Give me your name and——"

It was easy to tell from the expression on his face that the party at the other end of the line had hung up.

Sellers gave an exclamation of disgust, slammed the phone back into the cradle.

Four minutes passed. The telephone rang again. Sellers picked it up and said, "Hello."

This time the call was for Sellers. It was good news. A slow smile spread over his face. "Well, well, what do you know!" he said. "Well, what *do* you know?"

Sellers hung up the telephone and looked at me thoughtfully.

Abruptly the door started rattling. Somebody grabbed the knob from the outside and twisted it, jerked the door, then pounded on the panels.

"Who's there?" Sellers asked.

Bertha Cool's voice came from the other side of the door. "Let me in."

Sellers grinned, shot back the bolt and opened the door. "Come on in, Bertha," he said. "This is the Hazel Downer that I told you about. I told you I didn't want you monkeying around with her. Your partner has got you into a mess, but good."

"What's he done?" Bertha asked.

"For one thing," Sellers said, "your sweet little partner is mixed up in a murder."

"Who's dead?" Bertha asked.

"The man who was posing as Hazel's husband," Sellers said. "Hazel started living with him without benefit of clergy but with the benefit of everything else, including a damned good allowance. Then she started two-timing with a man named Herbert Baxley. Herbert Baxley's a stick-up artist. It may have been one of those cute little threesomes that you run onto in the mobs, where everybody is all hunky-dory—two men and a woman. On the other hand, it may have been business between Baxley and Downer.

"My present guess is that Standley Downer had fifty grand as his half of that armored truck job. It all begins to add up. When Herbert Baxley got a little alarmed he went into a phone booth and called a number. We thought he was calling Hazel, but it looks now as though he was calling Standley.

"We're running down a red-hot clue that a cute little trick by the name of Evelyn Ellis may have been the apex of another triangle. I've got men covering that now. When I get a report on that I may be able to find out where Donald picked up Standley Downer's trunk."

"His trunk?" Bertha asked.

"That's right," Sellers said. "Your little smart partner here somehow managed to palm off his trunk on Standley Downer."

Bertha turned to look at me with her hard, glittering eyes. Her face was a little more florid than usual but there wasn't the flicker of expression except in her hard eyes.

"What about that trunk, Donald?" she asked.

Sellers intervened. "Donald went to his place yesterday, Bertha. He was in a hell of a hurry. He threw some things in a trunk and beat it, carrying the trunk with him. A man that answered Donald's description bought a ticket on the Lark last night and checked a trunk. Now *you* start putting two and two together."

"You accusing him of murder?" Bertha asked.

"Why not?" Sellers said. "Standley Downer had some obligations with the fifty grand he'd picked up on that armored car job. He went to San Francisco. He intended to pay off some of his pressing obligations and then pick up Evelyn Ellis and go places and do things. He registered in the Caltonia Hotel. He had a suite. Evelyn was in that same hotel under the name of Beverly Kettle. Downer must have had this suite because he expected people would be calling on him. He undoubtedly had some business to attend to or he would have simply asked for a room. Actually, he'd wired ahead for a suite.

"When Standley Downer got to his suite, he found out he had the wrong trunk. The people who were expecting to collect from him thought his explanation was a little corny. They pulled everything out of the trunk, ripped out the lining, threw the clothes all over the joint ... and in the middle of all that was Standley Downer who had had a very flat thin carving knife stuck in his back—with no trace of the weapon. The murderer took that away with him.

"Now then," Sellers went on, "Donald is a smart little boy. He wouldn't come walking back into the arms of the police with any money on him. But a check with the air express companies shows that Donald bought some photographic goods in San Francisco. That package was sent down at Donald's request by air express with special handling instructions. So we called back to San Francisco and checked the photographic company that made the shipment and what do you know? A guy that answered Donald's description was in there this morning and bought a thirty-five millimeter camera, gave his card and insisted that the camera be packed and shipped by air express within an hour of the time he bought it, with special handling charges.

"Now, you know what we're going to do, Bertha? We're going right to your office and we're going to wait until that package comes in, and——"

"A package came in just as I left," Bertha said. "I wondered what the hell it was and started to open it and then your telephone call came in and I dropped everything and beat it over here."

"Where's the package now?" Sellers asked.

"Being wrapped to send back," Bertha said. "Nobody's buying cameras with partnership funds while I'm running the joint."

Sellers did some rapid thinking, turned to the other two, said, "All right, play it smart if you want to. It isn't going to buy you anything. If you don't want to talk, you don't have to. I searched Hazel Downer's apartment awhile back.

I'm going to search it again. This time it's going to be a *real* search.

"As soon as reinforcements show up, Donald, Bertha and I are going to take a little walk. We'll hold Hazel until we see what develops."

"You've got nothing on her," Ashby said. "I can get a writ."

"Keep your nose clean and you may spring her without a writ and in half the time," Sellers said. "Standley Downer wasn't murdered until this morning. I can tell within a couple of hours whether San Francisco wants her held or not."

"Where are *we* going?" Bertha asked Sellers.

"Down to your office," Sellers said.

"Then what?"

"We're going to look in Donald's little camera package," he said.

Bertha turned to me. "What the hell did you want a camera for, Donald?"

"To take pictures with," I told her.

Sellers chuckled, "You come with me and *I'll* show you what he wanted it for, Bertha."

Knuckles pounded on the door.

Sellers opened it. Two men stood on the threshold.

Sellers grinned and said, "This is Ashby. He's her attorney. This is Hazel Clune, alias Hazel Downer. Serve the search warrant on her and take this place to pieces, then go to her apartment and take it to pieces—I mean *really* take it to pieces.

"Come on, Donald. You and Bertha and I are going down to your office."

CHAPTER FIVE

FRANK SELLERS stopped the squad car in front of the office building, parking in a red zone, and said, "Camera supplies, eh, wise guy? Thought you were pretty smart, didn't you?"

Bertha barged out of the car, looking straight ahead, her jaw pushed out, eyes glittering, saying nothing to anybody.

We rode up in the elevator. Bertha stalked into the office and said to the receptionist, "Did you get that package wrapped to return to San Francisco?"

The girl nodded.

"Unwrap it," Bertha said.

Doris Fisher knew Bertha well enough not to argue. She opened a drawer, took out a pair of scissors and cut through the wrappings on the package which was addressed to the Happy Daze Camera Company in San Francisco.

Doris Fisher got the wrappings off the box. Sellers looked down at the excelsior-padded contents, fished out the thirty-five millimeter camera, looked it over frowningly.

"What's this?" he asked.

I said, "In our work we have to have photographs. This was a bargain and I bought it."

Bertha glared at me in speechless anger.

Sellers seemed puzzled, then his fingers explored farther down in the interior of the box. Suddenly his lips twisted in a grin. "Well, well, well," he said, and pulled out the box of five by seven enlarging paper. "What do you know?"

Sellers turned the box over in his hand, reached in his pocket, pulled out a penknife.

"Now look," I said, "that's enlarging paper. It can only be opened in a darkroom where there's absolutely no light. Otherwise you'll ruin it. If you want, I'll go in the closet where it's absolutely dark and open it and——"

"How nice," Sellers said. "We're going to open it right here in broad daylight. If there's anything in here that can't stand the light of day, Pint Size, we'll let *you* do the explaining."

66

Sellers started to cut the seals, then stopped, looked at the box thoughtfully, grinned and put his knife away.

"Of course, Donald," he said, "you couldn't have taken the paper out and put fifty grand in the box without cutting the seals. You did it very cleverly and with a very sharp knife so it hardly shows. Now, Bertha, I'm going to show you something about your double-crossing partner here."

Sellers pulled the lid off the box, disclosing the package wrapped in black paper on the inside.

"Don't open that black paper, Sergeant," I warned. "That's enlarging paper and light will ruin every sheet of it."

Sellers ripped the black paper off, threw it in the wastebasket, ripped off the inner wrapping of black paper and then stood goggle-eyed staring at the sheets of photographic enlarging paper.

I tried to hold my face without expression. It was a good thing Frank Sellers and Bertha were looking at the paper.

"Well?" Bertha said. "What the hell's so funny about this?"

Sellers picked up one of the sheets of paper, looked at it, inspected the shiny glaze of the uncoated side. He picked up three or four sheets and studied them separately.

"I'll be damned," he said.

I walked over and sat down.

Sellers hesitated a moment, then drove back into the box, pulled out every bit of excelsior, dumped it on the floor, turned the box upside down, tapped on the sides as though looking for a false bottom or something.

He looked up at Bertha. "All right," he said, "I should have known the little bastard would do something like that."

"Like what?"

Sellers said, "This is a dummy package, Bertha. Don't you get it? It's a decoy."

"What do you mean?"

"He was too smart to carry the fifty grand with him, Bertha, because he felt we might get wise to something and search him. He wanted the fifty grand shipped down here so it would be included in some legitimate business purchase he'd made up there. He's just that much smarter than you think he is. He knew that I might call at the office and ask you if any package had been received from San Francisco. You'd have said that a package had just come in and I'd have told you to bring it down to Headquarters or else I'd have come tearing up here and opened it.

"It's just like the brainy little bastard to have something like this darkroom paper that would be ruined when I opened it so he could have the laugh on me. Then he figured I'd have to dig up the price of a new box of enlarging paper out of my own pocket. Then, a couple of days later an innocent-looking package would come in from San Francisco. By that time the heat would be off and he'd just open the package, take the fifty grand and be that much ahead."

"You mean he's stealing fifty grand?" Bertha asked.

"Not stealing," Sellers said. "He's trying to get that fifty grand and make a deal with the insurance company."

"If you weren't so damned cocksure of yourself," I said, "you wouldn't pick up a button and sew a vest on it every time I start working on a case."

Sellers started chewing on his wet cigar.

"All right," Bertha said, "what do you want next?"

Sellers said, "I'm going to take Donald with me."

Bertha shook her head. "No, Frank," she said. "You can't do that."

"Why can't I?"

"You haven't got a warrant and——"

"Hell's bells," Sellers said, "I don't need a warrant. I've got him on suspicion of murder and half a dozen other things."

"Think it over, Frank," Bertha said in a low voice.

"Think what over?"

"The minute you take him down to Headquarters," Bertha said, "the reporters will be on your tail. There'll be a big story in the newspapers about how you've arrested Donald and——"

"Not arrested," Sellers said, "brought him in for questioning."

"He won't go unless you arrest him," Bertha said. "He's too damn smart for that. He'll get you to stick your neck out in public before you really have all the evidence and then make you look like a monkey while he winds up smelling like a rose."

Sellers chewed on the cigar for a few seconds, looked at me with angry eyes, looked at Bertha, started to say something, changed his mind, waited a few more seconds, then slowly nodded.

"Thanks, Bertha," he said.

"Don't mention it," Bertha commented.

Sellers turned to me. "Now look, wise guy," he said, "you make one move, just one move, and I'm going to give you the works. I'm going to throw the book at you and clobber you."

Sellers turned on his heel and swung out of the office.

Bertha said, "Donald, I want to talk with you."

"Just a second," I said, and walked over to where Elsie Brand was standing in the doorway of my reception office where she had been watching proceedings.

I said in a low voice, "Get me the Happy Daze Camera Company on the line. I want the manager. I'll probably be in Bertha's office when the call comes in. You ring me there but hold this guy on the phone so I can come back and talk in my office."

"Do you know the man's name?" she asked.

I shook my head. "He's Japanese. Just ask for the manager. I want him on the phone. They may be closed by this time. If they are, try and get a night number."

Elsie looked at me. "Donald, are you in trouble, *real* trouble."

"Why?" I asked.

She said, "The others were watching that camera box when Sergeant Sellers opened that box of paper. I was watching your face. You looked for a second as though you were going to fall down."

I said, "Never mind my face, Elsie. I've got myself in pretty deep and may have you along with me."

"Would I have to testify against you?" she asked.

"If they get you in front of the grand jury, you will. Unless . . ."

She watched me as I lapsed into silence.

"Unless we were married?" she asked.

"I didn't say that," I said.

She said, "I did. Donald, if you want to marry me so I can't testify and then go to Nevada and get a divorce afterward, it's okay with me. I'll do anything—anything."

"Thanks," I told her. "I——"

"Dammit to hell!" Bertha screamed across the office. "Are you going to stand there yakkity-yakking all afternoon or are you coming in here?"

"I'm coming in," I said.

I walked into Bertha's office. She closed the door, locked it and stuck the key in her desk drawer.

"What's that for?" I asked.

She said, "You're going to stay here until you come clean. I don't know what you were telling Elsie there in a low voice, but if you were telling her to call San Francisco and get the manager of that goddam camera store on the line, Bertha is going to sit right here and listen to every word you say."

"What makes you think I'm calling anyone in San Francisco?" I asked.

"Don't be a sap," she said. "Any time you go and buy a box of enlarging paper that's had the seals cut I want to know about it. All you bought that goddam camera for was so that you could include a box of photographic paper without arousing anyone's suspicions. Now what happened? Did that cameraman high-grade what you put in the box?"

I walked over to the window and stood with my back to Bertha, looking down at the street. I felt like hell.

"Answer me!" Bertha screamed at me. "Don't stand there trying to stall me. My God, don't you know you're in a jam? Don't you know I'm in a jam? I've never seen Frank Sellers like that in all my life and you haven't either. You——"

The telephone rang.

Bertha scooped up the receiver and said, "He'll take the call right here."

There was a moment of mumbled sound coming from the receiver, then Bertha yelled, "Goddammit, Elsie, I told you he'd take the call right here. Now, get that guy on the line."

I turned around and said, "I can't talk to him here, Bertha."

Bertha said, "The hell you can't. You talk to him right

here or you don't talk at all. Either pick up that phone and talk to the guy or I'm telling Elsie to cancel the call."

I turned and looked at the glittering anger in Bertha's eyes, walked over and picked up the telephone. "Is this the manager of the Happy Daze Camera Company?"

There was the rattle of quick, nervous, staccato Japanese accent on the line. "This is manager, Mr. Kisarazu."

"This is Donald Lam," I said, "in Los Angeles. Are you the man who sold me the camera and the enlarging paper?"

"That's right, that's right," he jabbered nervously into the telephone. "Takahashi Kisarazu, manager, Happy Daze Camera Company, at your service, please. What can I do, Mr. Lam?"

"You remember," I said, "that I bought a camera and a box of enlarging paper?"

"Oh, yes-s-s-s," he hissed. "Delivered already at airport. Sent specially to airport for rush handling express."

"The package is here," I said, "but the stuff I bought isn't."

"Package is there?"

"That's right."

"But stuff you bought not there?"

"That's right."

"Sorry, please, I do not understand."

I said, "I bought a special and particular box of enlarging paper. The box that came down here isn't the box I purchased. The seals had been tampered with on that paper. It had been opened."

"Opened?"

"Opened."

"Oh, sorry. So sorry. I have everything here on purchase slip. Will send new box of paper at once. So sorry."

"I don't want a new box of paper," I said. "I want the box I purchased."

"Don't understand, please."

"I think you understand too damn much," I told him. "Now, I want that box of paper that I purchased. The same one, understand?"

"Will be glad to send a new box right away, very quick, special handling charges. So sorry. Unfortunate accident.

71

Perhaps someone has opened box of paper after you made purchase, no?"

"What makes you think that?"

"Because of finding five by seven enlargement paper on floor by counter. Am very sorry. Excuse, please. We will make good."

"Now listen," I said, "get this and get it straight. I want that box of paper and I want it down here fast. If I don't get it, there's going to be trouble. Big trouble. You understand?"

"Yes, yes, plenty trouble already. So sorry about paper. Am sending box right away. Good-by."

He hung up the phone at the other end. I cradled the phone and met Bertha's eyes.

"Sonofabitch," Bertha said under her breath.

"Me?" I asked her.

"Him," she said. And then after a moment added, "You, too." Then she went on to say, "Dammit, Donald, you ought to know better than to try and outwit an Oriental. They can read your mind just like I can read the stock quotations in the newspaper."

"This was a wonderful buy in a camera," I said. "I think perhaps he smuggled it in."

Bertha's eyes were snapping. "Wonderful buy my eye," she said. "You didn't buy that camera because you wanted to take pictures. Now, why the hell *did* you buy it?"

"It might be better," I said, "if I didn't tell you. Maybe I'm in bad."

"Then *we're* in bad," Bertha said. "What was this evidence that you were trying to have sent down to you without anyone knowing about it?"

"It wasn't evidence," I said. "Frank Sellers was right. It was fifty grand."

Bertha's jaw sagged. Her eyes began to widen.

"Fifty ... grand ...!"

"Fifty grand," I said.

"Donald, you couldn't have! How in hell did you find it?"

"Sellers was right again," I said. "The guy was shipping a trunk. I juggled things so that I got his trunk and he got mine. The fifty grand was in his trunk. I just had a hunch that they might be laying for me, so I bought the camera and some enlarging paper. The box of enlarging paper had two packages of paper on the inside. I surreptitiously opened the box under the counter while the manager was getting some accessories for the camera I wanted and pulled out some of the paper and put the fifty grand inside the box. I said I wanted it shipped at once to the office here. I wanted a special messenger to take it to the air express so it would be here by the time I arrived."

"My God," Bertha said, "that's enough to have made the guy suspicious right there."

"No, it isn't," I said. "I did a lot of testing with the camera. I treated the paper as just a matter of course, nothing at all. The camera was the thing I seemed to be interested in. He was calling one of his clerks to rush it over to the air-express office when I left."

Bertha shook her head. "You're a brainly little bastard, Donald, and then at times you just knock yourself for a loop being too damn smart. Why the hell didn't you pick a store run by an American? You can't fool those Orientals. They bow and scrape and giggle, and all the time their shrewd little eyes are slithering around like a snake's tongue, seeing things that wouldn't mean anything to us but make us like an open book to them."

"You're provincial, Bertha," I said. "All nationalities have their individual mannerisms. The Japanese probably feel that we look each other straight in the eyes, shake hands, clap each other on the back with expressions of cordial sincerity and are lying like hell all the time. The oriental manners you describe are simply ceremonial. You're afraid of them because they can outthink you."

Bertha glowered at me angrily. "Go to hell," she said. "They didn't outwit me, they outwitted you."

"Well," I said, "there's no use arguing. You saw the package when it came in. Had it been tampered with?"

"Hell, no," Bertha said. "It was all sealed up nice and shipshape and it had this label from the camera store and was addressed to the firm for your attention. So I took it and opened it to see what it was. I never did find out. I just had the wrappers off when the phone rang and it was Frank Sellers, and so I beat it out there."

"Well," I said, "now we're really in the soup."

"In the soup!" Bertha exclaimed. "We're out of the frying pan and right in the middle of the fire. Somebody must have followed you, Donald. If it wasn't that damn Jap, somebody must have followed you and when you went into the camera store managed to be where he could watch you through a window or something. Then he probably intercepted the package some way and——"

Bertha caught the expression on my face. "What is it, Donald?"

"It was a woman," I said. "I remember that right after I went into the camera store a good-looking babe came in and started asking questions about cameras. She was down at another counter near the front of the store. I was in the used-camera department at the back end of the store."

"What did she look like?" Bertha asked.

I shook my head.

"Don't hand me that guff," Bertha said, suddenly angry. "A good-looking babe and you can't tell what she looked like?"

"Not this babe," I said. "I was too intent on making a substitution of that fifty grand while the Jap was out back getting cameras to show me. I wanted a camera and a case, too."

"All right," Bertha said after a while. "We've been taken. Now, you switched trunks. What happened to the trunk you got from Downer after you got the fifty grand?"

I said, "I paid rent on a room in the phony name of George Biggs Gridley. It's at the Golden Gateway Hotel. I left a teaser in my trunk so Downer would find it when he opened the trunk. That teaser would indicate that someone with the name of Gridley at the Golden Gateway Hotel was the owner of the trunk."

"What did you do that for?"

"I wasn't sure the money was in his trunk. I thought he'd fall for the gag the trunks had been mixed up by the railroad company and call Gridley at the Golden Gateway. I had things rigged so I could either take the call or fade out of the picture."

"Did Downer call?"

"No."

"Why?"

"Because he was dead."

Bertha thought that over. "How come the police didn't find the teaser and come barging down on the Golden Gateway Hotel looking for Gridley?"

"Because it wasn't there."

"Why not?"

"The killer took it."

"Good God!" Bertha exclaimed. "You've got the police after you for a murder and killers stalking you for fifty grand ... with some slick highgrading chick sitting pretty with our fifty grand stuck in her girdle."

"It looks that way," I admitted.

"Fry me for an oyster!" Bertha said.

Bertha sat silent for a while, then the thought of the money was too much for her. "Fifty ... thousand ... dollars," she said. "My God, Donald, you had the money in your hands! We could have got a fifteen-thousand-dollar reward. Why the hell did you let it slip through your fingers?"

"There's an angle I can't figure," I said. "There was a leak somewhere. Standley Downer knew Hazel had been in here."

Bertha said, "That Hazel Downer! *I'm* going to start working on her!"

"You leave her to me," I said. "She has confidence in me and——"

"Confidence in you!" Bertha screamed. "She's twisting you around her finger like a sap. She bats those eyelashes at you and smiles and crosses her legs and shows you a lot of nylon stocking and you just get down on the carpet and roll over.

"Dammit, can't you get *any* sense through your head? Don't you know women well enough to know that a man never gets to first base with a woman unless she's sized him up first, put the bat in his hand and given him a slow, easy pitch that's good for a safe hit? That babe has been twisting you right around her finger. Now, tell me the rest of the bad news."

I shook my head. "I'm doing this, Bertha."

"You're doing it?" she screamed. "Look what you've

done! You've got the agency in bad, you've got Sellers on the warpath, you're going to get yourself accused of murder and you damn well may get yourself convicted, for all I know. And, in the meantime, you've let fifty grand slip through your fingers. If you *don't* tell the truth you're licked and if you *do* tell the truth Frank Sellers is going to throw the book at you ... and then you have the crust to stand there and tell me to leave things to you. ... And with professional killers on your tail for high-grading the swag!

"I'm going to work on this Hazel babe down here. You get the hell back to San Francisco and don't let me see that smug-looking face of yours until you've brought back the fifty grand."

"Suppose," I said, "that Evelyn Ellis is the answer? What then?"

"Would you recognize that babe who followed you into the camera store?"

"I might," I said, "but I'm not certain. I doubt it. All I know is, she was young and easy on the eyes and smartly dressed."

"Now look," Bertha said, "she hung around there all the time you were there, is that right?"

"Yes, but she kept her back turned all the time."

"She was there when you went out?"

"Yes."

"You had to walk past her going to the door?"

"Yes."

"Can't you remember what she smelled like?" Bertha said. "A woman like that would have a little scent on and——"

I shook my head. "I can't remember."

"All right. I'll tell you one thing you can do," Bertha said. "You find out some way to get a picture of this Evelyn Ellis."

"I've got pictures of her," I said. "Pictures in a bathing suit, pictures in a ball gown, pictures in the near-nude and——"

"God almighty!" Bertha screamed at me. "Do I have to tell you how to be a detective? Take those damn pictures and beat it up to San Francisco. Go to that Jap photograph store. Find the man who was waiting on this babe, show him those pictures and ask him if that was the woman who was in there looking at cameras. If she's the same one you wire me and I'll come up and work her over. A good-looking leg and you're putty in their hands. Let 'em try showing *me* leg and I'll turn 'em over my knee. Now, for the love of Mike, get started before Sergeant Sellers gets wise and throws you in the clink."

I said, "Bertha, either I'm getting so I think like you or you're getting so you think like me, because that's exactly what I was planning to do."

"Well, get started," Bertha yelled. "Don't stand there telling me that we're seeing eye to eye for a change. My God, you've got me where I'm going to lose my license and you're just standing around here yakkity-yakking."

I started for the door.

I didn't dare to tell her the Japanese camera company had taken the publicity pictures of Evelyn Ellis. It was just as Bertha had said, I'd played myself for a sucker.

CHAPTER SIX

THE jet plane deposited me in San Francisco at seven-thirty P.M. I'd had a couple of complimentary glasses of champagne and a dinner. I took a taxi to the Palace Hotel, then did a little doubling around.

If they were following me it was such an artistic job I couldn't detect it.

When I had my back trail cleared I went to the Caltonia Hotel, went up to Room 751 without being announced and knocked.

After a moment I heard motion behind the door, a sort of rustling caution motion and then a woman's voice saying, "Who is it?"

"Open up," I said gruffly.

"Who is it?" she asked, and this time there was a note of alarm in her voice.

"Oh, for the love of Pete!" I said. "You should know my voice by this time. Open up."

I heard the bolt turn and the door opened.

"I'm sorry, Inspector," she said. "I didn't recognize your voice the first time. I——"

She did a double-take and started to close the door.

I pushed a foot against the door, then a shoulder, and came on in.

"You—who are you?"

"The name," I said, "is Lam. I'm an investigator."

"Oh, for heaven's sakes," she said, 'you're the man whose trunk——"

"Exactly," I said. "What I want to know is how he got hold of my trunk."

She had on pajamas, a silk creation of clinging cloth and vivid color. The top was unbuttoned down to the third button and the lower part of the pajamas had been tailored to show curves.

She was quite a dish, and she'd been crying.

She looked me over and said, "I'm sorry you came. The police have your trunk. There's nothing I can do for you."

"Where did all this happen?" I asked.

"On the tenth floor."

"When did it happen?"

"It must have been right after he arrived. He came in on the train and he had this suite reserved and——"

"Suite?" I asked.

"That's right."

"Why the suite?" I asked.

"That's the reservation he made over the telephone."

"But why a suite? Why not just a room?"

"You'll have to ask him," she said. "And there's not much chance of that now, is there?"

"Apparently not," I said.

"Sit down," she invited, and draped herself on a davenport, sizing me up with large limpid eyes that tried to look naïve and hurt but somehow seemed to contradict themselves. It was an expression of sinister innocence.

She said, "I understand you're working for that woman."

"What woman?"

"*That* woman—that Hazel Clune. She called herself Hazel Downer."

"You don't like her?"

"She's just a—a creature."

"We're all creatures."

"She's a gold-digger."

"How come?"

"You know, or at least you should know. She just latched on to Standley because she wanted money."

"He gave her money?"

"Of course he gave her money. That's why she ditched her regular boy friend and latched on to Standley. She milked him dry."

"What did she do with it?" I asked.

This time the eyes snapped fire. "You know what she did with it," Evelyn Ellis blazed. "She spent all she could get on glad rags, and then she stole fifty thousand more by switching the trunks. Then when poor Standley couldn't pay off they thought it was a stall and rubbed him out."

"Now," I said, "you're beginning to interest me."

"Thank you," she said sarcastically. "It's *so* seldom I interest men that it's a real thrill to have a big, strapping, stalwart, two-fisted hunk of a man like you tell me he's interested."

She yawned ostentatiously.

I said, "He had fifty thousand in his trunk?"

"He *did* have."

"And what happened to the trunk?"

"Hazel has it hidden away somewhere. She managed to switch your trunk so that he got the wrong trunk and then when he got here and opened it up and found he had the wrong trunk—well, then it was too late. He was ... involved."

"What do you mean, involved?"

"There were other people in with him and those people didn't like the way things were going."

"What do you mean, the way things were going?"

"He owed them money."

"That he hadn't paid?"

"That's what I told you. He couldn't pay. They thought he was stalling."

"He was intending to pay?" I asked.

"That's right."

"And he had fifty thousand?"

"At least that. Perhaps more."

"And where did this cash come from?"

She tilted her chin and looked down her nose. "*I* wouldn't know," she said demurely.

"Perhaps it would help if I did."

"And perhaps it wouldn't."

"Have you told the police any of this?"

"No."

"Why not?"

"They'll find out, and when they find out they'll have this Hazel creature dead to rights. If I tell the police and the police start running down that clue on my say-so, they'll think I was jealous and trying to frame her. She'd tell them that it was all a cockeyed story made up by a jealous rival and the police might fall for it and give her enough of a head start to let her cover her back trail.

"By not telling the police anything and playing it dumb, when the police get on her trail they'll go all the way before she has a chance to run to cover. I've answered the questions the police have asked and that's all. I haven't volunteered a thing."

I said, "You knew he was coming in here on the Lark?"

"Yes."

"Why didn't you meet him?"

"He didn't want me to."

"You knew he was going to have a trunk with him?"

"I knew he was bringing a large sum of cash with him so he could pay off. I didn't know it would be in a trunk."

"You knew he was going to stay at this hotel?"

She looked at me, moved slightly inside of the clinging silk so as to give her body a voluptuous sway, and said, "Look, Mr. Lam, I'm not a child, you know."

"You knew he had a reservation here?"

"Naturally."

"That it was a suite?"

"Yes."

"But you didn't go to the train to meet him?"

"He thought it would be too dangerous."

"He was going to call you after he got in?"

"Yes."

"But he never did?"

"No. The first I knew that he actually had arrived was when the police came. The chambermaid found his body." She whipped a piece of tissue from a container and dabbed at her eyes.

"What time was that?"

"I don't know the exact time—between two and three o'clock."

"Then there must have been several hours that you were wondering what had happened to him."

"I knew that he'd get in touch with me as soon as the coast was clear and I didn't want him to until the coast *was* clear."

"I understand the police think he was killed right around ten o'clock in the morning."

"The police haven't confided in me," she said.

"How did you know he had my trunk?"

"The police told me. They checked the cleaning marks on the clothing that was in there."

"I thought they didn't confide in you."

"They didn't. They were questioning me. They wanted to know everything I knew about you."

"What did you tell them?"

"All I knew."

"What was that?"

"Nothing."

I said, "This isn't going to do, Evelyn. You knew that he was here the minute he arrived at the hotel. You went up to join him in the suite. You were there when he opened the trunk, and then you found that it wasn't his trunk and that there wasn't any money.

"This man was pretty hot, otherwise he'd have carried the money in a money belt. When a man has fifty grand and is so afraid of being held up for it that he puts it in a trunk he has to be pretty hot.

"Now, I imagine at about the time he opened the trunk he told you to get down to the Southern Pacific Depot and tell them there'd been a mistake. You knew what this trunk looked like and you were to identify his trunk, tell them you'd put up a bond or anything that was required but they weren't to deliver that trunk to anyone else. Then you were to use a little bribery, a little sex appeal, and perhaps a little pull with some of the executives and try and get possession of the trunk.

"I have an idea you may have had a description of me. Anyway, you got there and became pretty well convinced that the trunk was gone, so then you started looking me up."

She yawned.

"Well?" I asked at length, as silence descended on the room.

She said, "I'm ready to have you go now."

"Or, *are* you?" I said. "Suppose *I'm* not ready to go now?"

She said, "I can call the house dick or I can call the police."

She yawned once more and patted her lips with polite fingers to mask the yawn.

"I may do a little calling myself," I said.

"Please do, Donald. Any time. The police will be very glad."

"What are *you* going to do now?" I asked.

"Go to bed—alone."

"I mean, do you have a job or——?"

She got up, walked to the door and held it open.

I settled myself in a chair, picked up a copy of *Hardware Age* that was on the table and started to read.

Evelyn stood there by the door for a few seconds, then came back, closed the door, said, "All right, if I can't do it the easy way, I'll do it the hard way."

"Attagirl!" I said. "I'm waiting for you to call the police."

"I will," she promised, "but I have a few things to do first."

She put her hand to the top of the pajamas and jerked down. A button popped and then a jagged tear appeared in the silk.

She devoted her attention to the lower part of the pajamas. "I always like to be able to show evidence of attempted assault," she said. "It makes a better impression on a jury."

I got up, took the magazine with me and made for the door.

"I thought you'd see things my way," she said. "And, by the way," she called after me, "send me a new pair of pajamas, Donald. You've ruined these."

I didn't even stop to look back.

I heard her throaty laugh and then the sound of the closing door.

I stopped by the clerk's desk and said, "I thought perhaps you'd like to have one of my calling cards."

I handed him a folded ten-dollar bill.

"It's certainly a pleasure to see you, Mr. Ten Bucks," he said. "You should show up more often. What can I do for you?"

"How many switchboard operators on daytimes?" I asked.

"What do you mean by daytimes?"

"Nine o'clock in the morning."

"Two."

"House calls," I said. "How are they divided? Any particular division?"

"Oh, yes. In periods of normal activity we divide at the sixth floor. The switchboard is so arranged that calls from rooms from the sixth floor on down are taken by the girl on the left and calls from the seventh floor on up are taken by the girl on the right."

"The girl on the right, mornings," I said, "is ... ?"

He said, "We wouldn't want to have any scandal; that is, no indication that girls listened in on conversations and divulged what they heard."

"Certainly *not*," I said. "You couldn't afford that and I couldn't afford it. It would be a crime. Now, the girl on the right—you have her name and perhaps her address?"

"That would be frowned upon," he said.

"I just want to talk with her for a while."

"You understand the hotel has been placed in a very embarrassing position on account of the murder."

"I understand," I said. "I wouldn't want to do anything that would cause any trouble or expose the hotel to any disadvantageous publicity."

As he continued to size me up, I added, "I'm the soul of discretion."

He scribbled a name and address on a piece of paper, pushed it face down across the counter, reached out and shook hands, and said, "It was a real pleasure to meet you. If you need anything up here again, remember that it's a pleasure to be of service."

"Thanks," I told him. "I'll remember."

I walked out, hailed a taxicab and looked at the paper the clerk had given me.

The name was Bernice Glenn and the address was an apartment house not too far out.

I settled back against the cab cushions, looked at my watch and did some mental arithmetic. I couldn't count on being very far ahead of pursuit. I had to make every minute count, but there was bound to be a period of inactivity between the time I exhausted the leads in San Francisco at night and the time the photographic store opened in the morning.

I put the cab on waiting time, took the elevator up to the third floor and knocked on the door of Bernice Glenn's apartment.

The door was opened a crack by a horse-faced young woman who seemed embarrassed when she saw me there.

"Bernie is out," she said.

"Who are you?" I asked.

"I'm Ernestine Hamilton, her roommate. We share the apartment."

"How did you know I wanted Bernie?"

"Why . . . they . . . I . . . well, I just assumed it."

She laughed in a high-pitched, nervous manner.

"Actually," I said, "I wanted to talk with both of you. How long before Bernie will be back?"

"She's on a date—you know what that means."

"Late?"

"Early."

"A.M. or P.M.?"

"A.M."

"May I come in and talk with you?"

"I'm in a mess. The apartment's a mess. I was cleaning up after dinner."

"I'm good at washing dishes."

"Not in an apartment of this size, you aren't. Two people in the kitchenette would cause collisions. Why do you want to see us both?"

"It's a long story," I said.

"Well, come on in and sit down. You can't wait for Bernie because that'll be too late and I need my beauty sleep, but I'll be glad to talk with you if you'll pardon me a minute."

She opened a closet door, grabbed some clothes off a hanger, shot into the bathroom and closed the door.

I looked out in the kitchenette. The smell of recent cooking clung to the place. The dishes had been washed and stacked on the sink but not rinsed or dried. There was a kettle of steaming hot water on the gas plate.

I rinsed out the dishes with hot water, picked up a dish towel, dried the dishes and stacked them.

I was just finishing up when I felt someone behind me and turned.

Ernestine Hamilton had taken off her glasses, had put on a cocktail gown and there was a heady trace of scent in the air.

"What in the world are you doing?" she asked.

"I've done it," I said, hanging up the dish towel. "What have you been doing?"

"I always change after dinner," she said. "Somehow it breaks the monotony. I ... you caught me unexpectedly. You shouldn't have done those dishes. What in the world? Who are you, anyway? What do you want?"

I carefully adjusted the folded dish towel on the rack, walked over to the davenport, took her arm and said, "I crave to talk, I want information."

"Who are you? You ... oh, I'll bet you're a police officer ... but you don't look the least bit like any police officer I ever knew."

"How many have you known?" I asked.

"Not very many," she said.

"Where?" I asked.

"Mostly on television."

"Were they real cops or actors?"

She laughed and said, "All right. I'll yield the point."

I said, "It's a temptation to ride along with the gag and let you go on thinking I'm an officer but I'm not. I'm a private detective."

Her eyes widened. "Ooh," she said, "a private eye!"

I looked over at the television set in the corner and made a little bow to it.

"What's that for?" she asked.

"For the build-up," I said. "Now tell me about Bernie."

"What about her?"

"What did she tell you about the dead man?"

"You mean the one that was murdered?"

"Yes."

"I ... why, should she tell me anything?"

"People in a hotel aren't exactly dumb, you know. They come pretty close to knowing that's going on. Now, was Evelyn Ellis expecting him this morning or not?"

"What's your name?" she asked.

"Donald," I said.

"No other name?"

"Donald does it," I said.

"I can't figure you, Donald."

"Don't try," I said. "Tell me about Standley Downer."

"I never saw him in my life."

"I know," I said. "Tell me what Bernie told you about him."

"What makes you think she told me anything?"

"It's a long story," I said.

"Could I hear it?"

"Well," I said, "you're interested in people. You're interested in things, but you don't wear your heart on your sleeve. You're not the kind of girl who goes out on casual dates and lets men paw you. When you give a man your friendship it means something."

She looked at me in surprise, then said after a moment, "What—what does all that have to do with Bernice?"

"Well, now," I said, "there's a peculiar situation. Bernice is just the opposite from you. Bernice likes to go out and have a good time. She likes to keep in the swim. Men don't mean very much to her except as escorts. She plays the field. She goes out with one one night and another the next night."

Her eyes narrowed. She said, "You're a detective. You're deducing all that from the fact that when I opened the door I immediately assumed you must be coming to see Bernice. I told you she was out before you asked for her. You've put two and two together. The fact that you are a stranger to me, that I assumed Bernice had made a date with you and that somehow had got her wires crossed on this particular night and had made two dates for the same night—you're just putting two and two together."

"Well," I said, "how did you expect me to know these things, by telepathy?"

"The way you . . . the way you read my mind."

"I wasn't reading your mind," I said. "I was studying character. Now, there's one thing about the sort of life you lead. You get rather lonely. You sit here in the evening and do some reading, but for the most part you watch television. You follow all the programs and have favorites on programs. You like the cops and robbers and you like the private eyes. I'll bet you tune in on all of them."

"I do," she admitted.

"All right," I told her, "that's the sketch. You're a girl who doesn't go out much but you're shrewd and you're interested in people. You're interested in television and there was a murder committed right in Bernice's hotel. You couldn't wait for Bernice to come home to find out what she knew about it."

Suddenly the girl threw back her head and laughed. "All right, Donald," she said, "you win. I pumped Bernice and turned her inside out."

"And what did you find out?" I asked.

"I don't know whether it's right to tell you or not. Some of it is very confidential. Some of it, things she's not supposed to tell."

"I know," I said. "Things she heard over the telephone."

"Donald, you're putting me in a spot."

I said, "Which would you rather do, team up with me in working on the case and swap information, or try to hold out on me and have me hold out on you?"

"I ... oh, Donald, *would* you let me work with you on the case?"

"If you've got some worthwhile information," I said. "How long has this thing been going on between Evelyn Ellis and Standley Downer?"

"No one knows," she said, "but it was long before she ever came to the hotel.

"She'd been living in Los Angeles in an apartment as Evelyn Ellis. About six weeks ago she came up here and registered in the hotel as Beverly Kettle. She kept her room by the month, but flew back and forth to Los Angeles.

"In Los Angeles she kept her apartment as Evelyn Ellis. She was building up two identities so that when she disappeared as Evelyn Ellis she had only to settle down here as Beverly Kettle."

"Who knew about this?" I asked.

"Apparently Standley Downer was the only one. He used to call her four or five times a day on the long-distance telephone when she would be up here.

"But Downer's girl friend, a girl named Hazel, found out about it some way. She came up here and there was a terrific scene, I guess. One of the adjoining rooms complained to the desk. There were very nasty words used."

"What sort of words?"

"Nasty words, slut and bitch, and ... oh, Donald, you

know how women are when they're fighting. They aren't at all careful of their language."

"All right," I said, "we'll pass the language for a while, but what about the murder itself?"

"Well, I guess when Standley Downer arrived he called her the first thing and she must have been up there for a while and then ... I guess that's when they discovered there was something wrong with the trunk or something."

"When did they start making calls?" I asked.

"Not a peep out of either of them. There was just silence from both the suite and her room."

"But he did call her when he arrived in the hotel?"

"After he got up in his suite. He called her then."

"And you think she went up?"

"I know she went up because somebody called for the suite and Bernie put the call through and Evelyn's voice answered."

"Do you know who made the call?"

"No, it was a man's voice that was on the line. As soon as he wanted to talk with Standley, why, Evelyn turned the phone over to Standley."

"And the conversation?" I asked.

She shook her head. "Bernie didn't have time to listen. There were calls coming in and she had to keep things moving across the board."

"No idea who it was that called?"

"No."

"Have the police talked with Bernie?"

"Not yet."

I took out my billfold and pulled out a twenty-dollar bill. "You're going to run into some expenses in this thing, Ernestine," I said. "I'd like to get a list of the numbers that Evelyn Ellis was calling during the last few days and I particularly would like to know whether she's been doing any business with the Happy Daze Camera Company and whether she's a nut on photography."

"Does it make any difference? In the murder, I mean?"

"It might make quite a lot of difference. Think you can find out for me?"

"Perhaps," she said. "Donald, how did you know all

those things about me, about my character? Am I that obvious?"

"You're not obvious," I said. "It's simply the lack of transparency that enables me to know you're deep and loyal and true and just a little bit lonely."

"Donald, you're trying to let me down easy."

"What do you mean?"

"I'm a wallflower," she said. "I know it, and you're smart enough to know it. You're smart enough to describe a wallflower so she sounds attractive. I don't know why I always team up with beautiful women as my roommates, but I do. I guess it's because I have some kind of self-punishment complex or something.

"Now, you take Bernie. She's out almost every night. She doesn't have any regular fellow. She plays the field and she keeps them all on the string. They're simply ga-ga over her.

"She likes to have me around because when she's going out I do the heavy end of the housekeeping. I like to have her around because early in the evening before she goes out, and while she's dressing for her date, I turn her inside out. I make her tell me all of the details of where she went the night before, what she did and all the conversation—all the passes the fellows made, how they went about it and everything.

"I pump her about her job, about what she's doing during the day. I make her give me all the gossip at the hotel and ... well, a less patient girl would throw me out on my ear. However, Bernie is a wonderful companion. She's very understanding, and, frankly, Donald, I think she understands me and knows that I'm suffering from some sort of a deep-seated frustration. I can't live the kind of life I want myself and so I live a vicarious existence."

"What do you do, Ernestine?" I asked.

"A bookkeeper," she said. "I *would* have to study bookkeeping! Of course, I had some secretarial training, too, but I like figures and figures like me. I write a neat hand, I add columns of figures accurately, I can play tunes on an adding machine while I'm reading figures off a column. I play the adding machine by touch and never make a mistake.

"That's another thing about me. The other girls, who are secretaries, doll themselves up in good-looking clothes, take dictation from the boss and he notices them. He's not offensive about it, but he sure notices when the girls have on nice-looking clothes. But a bookkeeper gets tucked away in a corner and no one ever notices what she's got on.

"That's me. That's my niche in life."

"You know what?" I told her.

"What?"

"You would make a jim-dandy female detective."

"I would?"

I nodded.

"Why?"

"Well, in the first place, you don't stand out too much. The very qualities that you've been complaining about that cause you to be pushed back into a corner somewhere in an office would be ideal for detective work. You could get around without being noticed. You're good at deduction and you have remarkable powers of observation. You have a retentive memory and you're a pretty good judge of character—including your own.

"When I get back to Los Angeles I'm going to look around and see what I can find down there. The next time we have a case where we can use a woman operative I'm going to see if you want to get out of this bookkeeping niche and really get into the swim of life."

"Would that mean quitting my job up here?" she asked.

I nodded. "How much of a sacrifice would that be?"

"Not too much."

"You could get another job in case it didn't pan out?"

"I could get a job anywhere any time. What's your real name?"

I gave her one of my cards. She handled it as though it had been printed on platinum.

"How long have you been working at your present job?" I asked.

"Seven years."

"Exactly," I said. "You're the type that keeps things running quietly and efficiently. That's the reason Bernice likes to have you in the apartment. You keep things spick-and-span. I'll bet that Bernice runs out about half the time leaving clothes scattered around the place and when she comes back she finds the bed turned down, her clothes all folded and put away—and I have an idea you do the same thing around the office. I think you pick up after the other girls. I think you cover up their mistakes. I think you keep things running with such quiet efficiency that nobody reallys knows you're on the job. All they know is that whenever they want information it's there on their desks neatly typed, accurate, and produced at a moment's notice.

"I have an idea that if you quit and they tried to hire someone to take your place, the whole shebang would go into chaos. People would be running around tearing their hair and the boss would be saying, 'What the hell happened to Ernestine? Get her back. No matter what you have to pay, get her back.'"

Ernestine looked at me, and her eyes began to blaze with enthusiasm. "Donald," she said, "I've often wondered about that myself, only I've put the thought out of my mind and felt that I was just too conceited."

"Conceited, nothing!" I told her. "Why don't you make the experiment?"

"Donald, I'm going to do it. I've got some money saved up. I can get along for a while and ... I'm giving my notice tomorrow."

"Now, wait a minute, sister," I said. "Let's take it easy. Let's not go completely overboard with the first wave that comes over the deck and——"

"No, Donald, I'm going to do it. I've been thinking it over in the back of my mind. I didn't realize how much I have been dreaming about doing it until ... oh, *Donald*!"

She had her arms around my neck and was squeezing me up against her with all her strength. I could feel the muscles quivering underneath the dress.

"Donald," she said, "you dear, you darling! I'm going to start showing you what I can do, right tonight! When Bernice gets back I'll get every blessed scrap of information about that murder and all the gossip from the hotel. I'll milk her dry."

I held her tight and patted her hips. "Good girl," I said.

She took a deep breath and just lay quiet in my arms, her eyes closed, a smile on her lips. I'd caught her at exactly the right moment. She'd been building to this crisis for months and now suddenly she made a decision and was on Cloud Seven.

She promised she'd plead a headache and duck out on her job tomorrow; that would leave her free to help me.

She couldn't stop trembling from the excitement.

It was eleven o'clock when I checked in at a Turkish bath to spend the night. I had an idea the police might be combing the hotels for me, but I didn't think they'd bother looking into a Turkish bath.

I was careful to give my right name and address.

CHAPTER SEVEN

I HAD a leisurely breakfast of fruit juice, ham and eggs, coffee and hot cakes. I wanted to have a good meal aboard because I didn't know when I was going to get the next meal.

The Happy Daze Camera Company opened at nine o'clock. I went through the doors at one minute past nine.

I saw the lenses of horn-rimmed spectacles, a flashing set of teeth, and the Japanese who had sold me the camera was smothering me with politeness.

"So sorry," he said. "I am Takahashi Kisarazu. Much trouble. Somebody throws enlarging paper on floor. Must have been from package of paper you bought. Excuse it, please. So sorry."

He bowed and smiled and smiled and bowed.

"We're coming to that in a minute," I said. "Where's your partner?"

Takahashi Kisarazu nodded to a wooden-faced Oriental who was arranging cameras in a showcase.

"Get him over here," I said.

Kisarazu rattled out staccato syllables and the other man came over.

I opened my wallet and showed two of the small pictures of Evelyn Ellis. "You know this girl?" I asked.

He studied the pictures for a long, long time.

I looked up quickly. Takahashi Kisarazu was looking at him in a peculiarly intent manner.

"*I* take pictures," Kisarazu said.

"Sure," I said, "you take picture. Your name is on here and the name of this company is stamped on the back. You know this girl."

"But of course," he said. "Publicity pictures. I have studio in rear, portrait photography. You like see?"

"You know this girl," I said.

"Yes, of course," Kisarazu said. "I know."

"You know where she lives?"

"I have address in my file records. Why you ask about this picture, please?"

I turned to the partner. "When I was buying my camera in here," I said, "there was a young woman in here. Was that this woman in the picture?"

He held his head completely motionless for about a second. His eyes slithered over to Takahashi Kisarazu, then he shook his head.

"No," he said, "different girl from one in picture."

"Do *you* know that customer? Have *you* ever seen her before?"

"So sorry. I do not know. She look at camera, she ask questions, but she does not buy camera."

"How long did she stay after I left?"

"You go out, she go out."

"Right away?"

"Almost same time."

I faced Kisarazu. "Now look," I said, "I don't know all the ramifications of this thing, but before I get done I'm going to find out. If you're trying to——"

I saw his eyes look past my shoulder and the fixed smile which had been on his face became a frozen grin.

"Okay, Pint Size," Sergeant Sellers' voice said, "this will button it up."

I turned to look at him.

Sellers had a plain-clothes man with him. I knew before he told me that this was a San Francisco police officer.

"Okay," Sellers said, "we're taking over from now on, Donald. You're just coming along with us. They want to see you up at Headquarters."

"On what charge?" I asked.

He said, "It'll be larceny at the start and murder before we get through."

Sellers turned to Kisarazu. "What was this fellow trying to find out?" he asked.

Kisarazu shook his head.

The man with Sellers pulled back the lapel of his coat, showed his badge. "Start talking," he said.

"Try to find out about pictures taken of model," Kisarazu said.

Sellers frowned. "He wasn't trying to get you to clam up about what happened when he bought the cameras?"

"What do you mean, clam up?"

95

"About tampering with the photographic paper?"

"Oh, paper," Kisarazu said, and smiled. "Very funny." He let his smile become a snicker.

"Somebody is opening package of enlarging paper underneath counter," Kisarazu said. "Very funny. After Mr. Lam leaves store we find enlarging paper on floor— seventeen sheets, double weight, white glossy. Same brand Mr. Lam buying at the time he stand at counter and I go look for cameras."

Kisarazu bowed several times as though his head had been a cork bobbing on the water.

"Well, I'll be go-to-hell," Sellers said.

Kisarazu kept on bowing and smiling.

Sellers reached a sudden decision. "Okay, Bill," he said to the man with him, "you take this guy to Headquarters and hold him. I'm going to shake this place down. There's something here . . . the brainy little bastard."

The man he had addressed as Bill clamped viselike fingers on my biceps. "Okay, Lam," he said, "let's go."

He lowered his shoulder and started me toward the door.

I went along because there was nothing else to do.

Behind me I could hear Kisarazu's parting remark, "So sorry, Mr. Lam," he said, "so sorry."

CHAPTER EIGHT

I was kept waiting at Headquarters for more than three quarters of an hour before Frank Sellers came in, and then I was taken into one of those dispiriting rooms so characteristic of police headquarters.

A battered oak table, some brass spittoons on rubber mats, a few plain straight-backed chairs and a calendar on the wall constituted the only furniture. The linoleum on the floor looked as though it was covered with caterpillars, each caterpillar being a burn varying from one to three inches in length, where cigarettes had been flipped casually in the direction of the spittoons and had missed.

The man whom Frank Sellers had addressed as Bill turned out to be Inspector Gadsen Hobart. He didn't like the name with which he had been christened, everyone knew it and, as a courtesy, called him Bill.

Sellers kicked out one of the straight-backed chairs away from the table and pointed to it. I sat down.

Inspector Hobart sat down.

Frank Sellers stood looking down at me, nodding his head at me as though saying, I always knew you'd turn out to be a crook and by George, I wasn't disappointed.

"All right, Pint Size," Sellers said at length, "what have you got to say for yourself?"

"Nothing."

"Well, you'd damn soon better think of something because right now we've got a murder rap pinned on you so tight even you can't squirm out."

I didn't say anything.

"We don't know *how* you did it," Sellers said, "but we know *what* you did. You switched trunks with Standley Downer. You got his trunk, you found the false bottom in it, you picked up fifty grand, maybe more, but fifty for sure.

"Now then, I don't pretend to know exactly what happened after all. All I know is that you had fifty grand that was so hot it was like a stove lid. You had to find someplace to conceal it. You were afraid that somebody was going to frisk you before you got out of town, so you went to that camera store. You bought a camera and that gave you an excuse to get some enlarging paper. You opened the box of enlarging paper and spilled some sheets on the floor, then you submitted the fifty grand in place of the photographic paper you'd slipped out and told Kisarazu to ship the whole thing to your office in Los Angeles. You figured no one would ever think of opening a box of enlarging paper.

"Now then, somebody double-crossed you. That was the weak point in your scheme. You didn't have enough time to cover your tracks, so somebody got onto those tracks and didn't lose any time once he got started.

"Apparently this person had some dame shadow you into the photographic store and then they managed to open the package long enough to pull out the bills, or it was tampered with before it left the store—and I'm not giving that Jap a clean bill of health—not yet."

I said, "I take it all of this makes me guilty of murder."

"It helps."

"Yesterday," I said, "you were thinking that was a plant and the business at the camera store was just a decoy. What made you change your mind?"

"I'll tell you what made me change my mind," Sellers said. "We covered all the express offices up here and the postal offices to see if any more packages had been sent to you—and what do you think we found?"

"What did you find?"

"We found lots of things," Sellers said. "We found a package of books and cards that had been sent to you by yourself. And you know what we think? We think those books and cards came out of Downer's trunk."

"And proof?" I asked.

"We're getting it," Sellers said. "Don't rush us. Just give us time. Here's something else we found out that you don't know. We found the cabinet maker that Downer hired to put a false bottom in his trunk. That little piece of information jolted you, didn't it, Pint Size?

"A man doesn't put a false bottom in a trunk unless he intends to conceal something in it, so we're pretty certain something was concealed in Downer's trunk. And knowing what we're after, we know what it was—fifty grand in hot money. So since we know that Downer had your trunk we're pretty certain that you had Downer's trunk. These cards and things are probably in Downer's handwriting. We've got the best handwriting expert on the Coast working on that stuff right now. If that turns out to be in Downer's handwriting it ties you right in with Downer and the missing trunk, and that ties you in with the missing fifty grand, and that ties you in with murder.

"Now I don't think you were intending to go south with the fifty grand. I think probably you were planning on making a deal with the insurance company so you could get a reward. I told you to lay off. I warned you this was something I was going to handle myself, but you wouldn't listen to me. You had to go ahead on your own. Now then, you're tied up to your neck in a murder case.

"Personally, I don't think you murdered Downer. I don't think you're the type. Frankly, I don't think you have the guts.

"I'm going to give you just one break—one more chance. You start talking and come clean, tell the whole thing so it makes sense, and if I figure it's on the up and up we'll sit tight for a little while before we throw the murder rap at you. I still think that murder was committed by someone else, but I'd bet ten to one that you got the fifty grand."

Inspector Hobart hadn't said a word. He was sitting there sizing me up, watching my every motion.

I said, "Suppose you quit using me for a punching bag for a while and let's talk a little sense."

"No one's used you for a punching bag," Sellers said. And then after a significant pause, added, "Yet."

I ignored the comment and said, "You solved an armored car theft of a hundred grand. You came up with fifty grand. The thief says you got a hundred. That leaves you on the spot. What you want is to prove this guy a liar and that you never had but fifty grand.

"About the only way you can do that is to find out who *did* have the extra fifty grand and come up with it. Then you can make Baxley eat his words."

"Keep talking," Sellers said. "I always like to hear you talk. Every time I listen I get stung, but I like to listen just the same. It's like taking tranquilizers."

"The hell you get stung," I said. "Every time you've listened to me so far you've come out on top of the heap."

Sellers said, "You always used me to get something you wanted."

"And always *gave you* something *you* wanted," I said.

"Keep talking," Sellers said. "I've got other things to do besides argue with you."

I said, "If what you say is right, Herbert Baxley and Standley Downer arranged to hoist a hundred grand out of that armored truck. That right?"

"Right."

"All right, how did they know what to look for? How did they know which truck had the dough and how did they know there was a hundred grand in thousand-dollar bills?"

"They could have had a tip-off. They could have been on a blind."

"The only way you can save your skin," I told Sellers, "is by *proving* that Standley Downer was the other partner. Even if you should show up with fifty grand now and say that you had recovered it from Downer or from me, they'd laugh at you. They'd think that you had stashed it away someplace and had dreamed up a good story to help you out of a tight corner when the situation got too hot for you."

"*You* think about saving *your* skin," Sellers said. "I'll worry about saving mine."

I said, "*If* your hunch is correct, Baxley and Downer had the money long enough to make a two-way split. Therefore, Downer knew you'd corralled Baxley and felt Baxley would talk, and so he took his fifty grand and got out in a hurry."

"You haven't said anything so far," Sellers said.

"Now, once more assuming that what you're deducing is correct," I went on, "I come back to the fact—how did they know that hundred grand was going to be on that particular truck, and how did they know it would be where they could get at it?"

"Your needle's stuck," Sellers said. "You've been all over that once before."

"No, I haven't. You say you found a secret compartment had been built in Downer's trunk. Therefore, Downer got the trunk first and it wasn't until later that he planned to get what he was going to put in it—fifty nice new thousand-dollar bills that would lie flat on the floor of the hidden compartment. He had the whole thing planned long before that armored truck ever picked up the money."

Sellers frowned, then flashed a quick glance to Inspector Hobart.

Hobart, without taking his eyes off of me, said, "He's got something there, Sellers."

"All right," Sellers said to me, "go on, Pint Size. Talk your fool head off. I'll listen. When you get done you'd better have something that amounts to fifty grand, otherwise you're going to be out of circulation for a long, long time."

I said, "It was well planned and Downer was in on the play from the start. Downer knew that a certain private detective was going to be on his trail because his wife, or Hazel Clune, if you prefer that name, had consulted that detective. Downer knew that Hazel knew about the hiding place in the trunk. Therefore, it wasn't safe any more. So Downer decided to keep the money in a money belt on his person.

"Downer came to San Francisco. He wanted everyone to think he'd lost the fifty grand. Therefore *he* switched things deliberately so he'd get my trunk. The scheme worked. That was a trick taken by Downer. It fooled you and it fooled everybody except one person."

"Who?" Sellers asked, frowning thoughtfully.

"The murderer. Now, if *you* want to get off the spot *you* only need to prove Baxley actually did have a partner. That lets *you* out."

Sellers started rubbing the angle of his jaw with the fingers of his left hand.

Inspector Hobart said to Sellers, "The guy's right, Frank. *You* get off the spot when you can prove Baxley had a partner. *I* get off the spot when I've found the murderer."

"You've got him," Sellers said.

"Maybe I have and maybe I haven't," Hobart said.

Sellers said, "You can hold him on suspicion."

Hobart shook his head. "As a material witness, is all."

"I'm for calling in the press," Sellers said. "I'd book him on suspicion of murder."

Hobart thought it over for a moment, then said, "I don't

like it, but if it'll help you personally, we can stand the gaff."

I said to Inspector Hobart. "There should have been some clues there in the room where Downer was murdered."

Sellers grinned. "Listen to him now. He's telling *you* how to investigate a homicide."

The Inspector motioned Sellers with his hand to keep quiet. "What sort of clues, Lam?" he asked.

I said. "The guy was stabbed in the back."

"That's right."

"Fell forward on his face."

"Right."

I said, "If somebody was putting a lot of pressure on Downer, he'd hardly have turned his back on them."

"Maybe he didn't know the other person was in the room," Sellers said.

"Maybe," I agreed.

Inspector Hobart was interested. "Keep talking," he said. "What do you think happened?"

I said, "Downer had just finished opening the trunk when he was killed."

"Why was he opening the trunk when he knew it wasn't his trunk?" Inspector Hobart asked.

"That," I said, "is what I'm telling you. How do you know *he* didn't switch trunks? Why did he get killed as soon as it became apparent someone *had* switched trunks?"

"You got the answer to that question?" Hobart asked.

"I may have," I said.

"You're in San Francisco now," he said. "The extent to which you come out of this, if you do come out of it without losing a lot of hide, will be measured by the extent to which you co-operate with the San Francisco police."

"That," I said, "depends on what you mean by co-operation."

"When we co-operate up here we do a reasonably good job," Hobart said.

"Watch him," Sellers warned. "He's a smart little bastard and he'll out-trade you if you give him a chance."

I said, "Let's concede that Standley Downer had a trunk made. He had a secret compartment in it. He wanted to use that secret compartment for storing fifty nice new one-thousand-dollar bills. Now then, where did he intend to get those bills?"

"Go on, wise guy," Sellers said. "You're telling the story. We've got lots of time. Tell us, where did he expect to get the fifty one-thousand-dollar bills?"

"He expected to highjack them," I said.

"From Baxley's partner."

"Baxley's partner!" Sellers exclaimed. "What are you talking about? Standley Downer was Baxley's partner."

"What makes you think so?"

"Everything points to it. The fact that Baxley got in a panic and called Hazel Downer and ... when he knew we were following him ..."

Sergeant Sellers' voice, which had started out full of confidence, began to lose some of its assurance and finally trailed away into silence.

"Exactly," I said. "You've made the one mistake an investigator should never make. You've started out with an assumption and then you've tried to twist the evidence to support that assumption."

"All right," Sellers said. "What do *you* think?"

"I think," I said, "that Baxley was smarter than you thought he was."

"Go ahead."

"Baxley and his partner both knew that Downer was a dangerous man, that he was on to what they were doing. When Baxley found out you were following him he deliberately led you to Hazel Downer. She was the red herring he wanted to draw across your trail so you wouldn't get wise to his real partner."

"All right, Pint Size," Sellers said, trying to appear jaunty, "I am tuning in on your broadcast so you may as well go ahead with the commercial. Who was the partner?"

"I don't know."

Sellers' face began to get red. "You mean you've taken me all around the rosebush in order to tell me that you don't know where you're going?"

I shook my head. "I know who I *think* he is."

"Who?"

"Dover C. Inman, the proprietor of the Full Dinner Pail.

I was laying a foundation to go to work on him when you muscled in and gummed up my play."

"What's the Full Dinner Pail got to do with it?" he asked.

I said, "You had all the knowledge in your possession right from the start. You just didn't use your head. You made the mistake of being decoyed by a red herring and ..."

"Never mind playing that same old tune," Sellers said. "I've heard it so much I'm sick of it. Never mind my mistakes, smart guy. What makes you think Inman is the one that had the money?"

"Because," I said, "Baxley went there and got some sandwiches and had them put in a paper bag. Then he sat and ate the sandwiches and put the paper bag in the trash box. Why did he do that?"

"Because he found out we were watching him."

I shook my head and said, "After you and your partner followed him out of the drive-in, he found out you were watching him. Everything he did up to that point was pre-arranged."

"Then why did he put sandwiches in a bag, and then eat them?"

"Because he had to have a bag so he could put his partner's fifty grand into the trash box where the partner could get it. He made the switch right under your nose and you were too dumb to get it. Then when you nabbed him, he said you'd taken the whole hundred thousand because he *had* to give his partner time to get the money and hide it in a safe place."

"What the hell are you talking about?" Sellers asked, but there was just a trace of panic in his voice.

I said, "Look at it this way. If Baxley had ordered those sandwiches to take out, he'd have taken 'em out unless he saw you and became panic-stricken. If he saw you and became panic-stricken, he wouldn't have eaten the sandwiches. He'd have mushed them up a bit and put them in the bag and thrown them away. But he sat there and *ate* the sandwiches, cool as a cucumber. *Then* he threw the paper sack in the trash container, wiped his hands on a napkin, got in his car and started to drive away. Then he spotted you and that was when he decided to drag Downer in as a decoy.

"Put yourself in Baxley's place. Suppose you were dialing a number and you looked back and saw some officers watching you. Remember, you're an old hand at the game. You're a two-time loser. Would you drop the receiver, dash out and jump in a car and try to outrun a squad car from a standing start?

"You'd have done nothing of the sort. You'd have turned back to the telephone and, when someone at the Downer place answered, said, 'Hold everything. I think some cops are on my tail. You'd better take it on the lam.' Then you'd put in another dime and dial another number, pretend to talk for a while, hang up, stretch, yawn, and walk leisurely out of the telephone booth.

"You were either going to pick him up or you weren't. If you were going to pick him up, there was nothing he could do about it. All of that panic stuff was an act he was putting on so that you wouldn't go back to the one place where he didn't want you to go—that trash box at the Full Dinner Pail.

"Everything points to the Full Dinner Pail in this thing. That's where the job was pulled. That's where the truck drivers of that armored car stopped all the time for a coffee break.

"Of course, I'm not sure it was Inman, the proprietor, who was in on it. It could have been one of the girls, but for my money, it was somebody there at the Full Dinner Pail and that fifty grand was put in the bag that had contained the hamburger sandwiches when Baxley dropped the bag into the container."

Sellers looked at Inspector Hobart.

Inspector Hobart nodded, almost imperceptibly.

"Suppose I buy this thing," Sellers said. "Then what?"

"I don't care whether you buy it or not," I said. "I'm just telling you the way it looks to me."

"All right, then, how did it happen Hazel Downer had your name in her purse?"

"She didn't have my name. She had the name of Cool and Lam, both of us. Actually, she wanted to find out if Standley was two-timing her with a babe by the name of

Evelyn Ellis, who had won a few beauty contests and was making a play for Standley. Hazel wanted to know where she stood. So she decided she'd just have someone do a shadow job on Downer. She looked through the classified phone directory. Our names looked good—COOL AND LAM. She copied them on a piece of paper. She wanted to hire us to find out if she was the low babe on the totem pole or whether Standley was feeling his oats enough to do a casual job of cheating on the side which wouldn't mean a thing."

Sellers looked inquiringly at Inspector Hobart.

Hobart laughed and said, "All right, Frank, if you want my opinion the guy's handing us a line of fact and fiction. The parts he wants us to lay off of he's lying about. On the drive-in business he's giving you a valuable idea."

"How do you figure it?" Sellers asked. "You got any real proof?"

"Hell, no," Hobart said, "only I've been years on this job. I get so I can tell when they're lying and when they're telling the truth. This guy is doing both."

Sellers turned to me. "I'm not going to be a sucker. I'm going to look into this. I'm going to think it over. But this song and dance isn't going to do *you* any good. *You're* going to be sitting in a cell."

I shook my head, "No, I'm not."

"That's what you think," Sellers said. "You try and spring yourself out of this and you're going to have a surprise."

"I'm not going to try to spring myself," I said, "and I'm not going to have a surprise. But I'm going to send for an attorney and after I get an attorney I'm going to have a press conference and I'm going to yell frame-up so loud that some of it is going to stick."

"What do you mean, a frame-up?" Sellers asked.

"Draw your own conclusions," I said. "Down in Los Angeles you're in bad. Baxley says that you recovered a hundred grand. You say there was only fifty grand there. That makes a stink. You're looking for an out, so you come up to San Francisco and try to nail me on a frame-up so as to take the heat off yourself."

"You'd do that to me?" Sellers asked.

"If you throw me in the clink, I'll do that to you," I told him.

"Why, you little insignificant rat! You puny little nincompoop! I'd break you in two!"

"No, you wouldn't," I said. "This is San Francisco. They've got troubles of their own. They're not going to get in bad over your trouble in Los Angeles. Inspector Hobart has got a murder to solve."

"And I suppose it's your idea you can help me out on that," Hobart said.

"That's right," I told him.

"The brass of the bastard," Sellers said.

I said, "Wait a minute. I'm not trying to hurt you, Sergeant, unless I have to. And I'm not going to try to do Hobart any good unless I have a chance to play my hand in my way. Now then, you want me to talk. I've talked. Now I demand a lawyer."

Sellers reached out, and slapped my face hard with the palm of his right hand, then slapped it on the other side with the back of his right hand as he cuffed the hand back.

"Why, you little——"

Hobart's voice was cold and hard. "Hold it, Sergeant!"

There was something in Hobart's voice that caused Sellers to freeze.

"I think we'd better talk," Hobart said. "I've got some ideas myself."

"Don't let him sell you," Sellers warned angrily. "The little bastard is smart. I admit that."

"If he's that smart he can make us trouble," Hobart said, "and if he's that smart he can do us some good. I've got an idea. Come on in here. I want to talk."

He turned to me and said, "You stay right there, Lam. Don't move."

They left the room.

I was left alone for about fifteen minutes. Then Inspector Hobart entered the room, drew up a chair at the table, opened a package of cigarettes, offered one to me, took one himself, lit up, settled back, inhaled deeply, then let the smoke come out of his throat as he spoke so that the words seemed wrapped in a smoky aura.

"Lam, you're a liar," he said.

107

I said nothing.

"And it's damned skilful lying," he went on. "You've mixed some truth and some lies all up together. I know what you've said is both false and true, a mixture of logic and crap. And I don't know which is which."

I kept silent.

"The annoying thing," he said, "is that you must think the police are a terrible bunch of saps. You know, some fellows could get themselves in quite a bit of trouble trying to pull the type of stuff you've been trying to pull."

I just sat there.

He looked up at me and grinned and said, "And the funny part of it is, I don't give a damn."

There was silence for a few moments. Then he took another deep drag at the cigarette and said, "The reason I don't give a damn is because somehow I have a feeling that you're on our side all the way through but you're in so deep yourself you can't take us into your confidence, and what you're trying to do is to get enough slack on the rope so you can get out and clean this thing up before you get jerked off your feet. *I* think you had the fifty grand and lost it and want to get it back.

"Now then, Sergeant Sellers is in a bind. That's one of the things that can happen in police work. He's got to get out of it as best he can. Somehow I have an idea you've given him a lead that may amount to something.

"I'll tell you what I'm going to do with you, Lam. I'm going to let you walk right out that door. I'm going to give you the keys to San Francisco. I'm going to let you just prowl around on your own. Only understand that if you stub your toe and get into trouble you're going to be in trouble just as deep as though I'd never seen you in my life. In fact, I'll let the other boys handle it. I'll be home abed or watching TV or something. You get that?"

I nodded.

"Now," he said, "I've got a homicide to clean up. I'm going to give you lots of rope and let you stir around because I think perhaps you're going to uncover some evidence.

"I don't know what your game is, but I have an idea it isn't solving a homicide. Personally, I think you're in this thing a lot deeper than you're letting on and *I* think you're sweating because you've taken a chance with fifty grand in hot dough and someone has outsmarted you.

"However, I'll tell you one thing. You've got enough brains to make a lot of trouble for Sellers in case you decide to do so. We haven't got enough of a case to pin a homicide on you, and if we try to detain you and you blow the whistle on Frank Sellers and say that he's using you as a patsy to cover up, you can get lots of publicity up here because this isn't Sellers' hometown and the papers here like to throw mud on Los Angeles.

"For your confidential information, Sellers has left for the airport. He's taking a plane back to Los Angeles. I think you'd better keep away from the airport until after Sellers gets started. Sellers is pretty much put out. I had to do quite a bit of talking before he was ready to listen.

"You understand?"

I nodded.

Inspector Hobart jerked his thumb to the door. "Get the hell out of here," he said. "And just remember a couple of things. One of them is that I have a homicide to solve; the other one is that you're a private detective who has his own troubles—and those troubles could get worse.

"If you run onto any homicide evidence I want to know about it."

"Where can I get you?" I asked.

He took a card out of his pocket, scribbled a couple of numbers on it and slid it across the table to me. "One of those numbers will get me any hour of the day or night," he said.

"How anxious are you to get this thing cleaned up?"

"Just as anxious as any man could be for anything," he said. "I'm so damned anxious that I stuck my neck out with Sergeant Sellers. I'm so damned anxious that I'm giving you a break when I have a feeling that I should take you across my knee and give you a good walloping in order to teach you that the police aren't the damn fools you seem to think they are.

"Now then, does that answer your question?"

"It answers it," I said.

I got up and started for the door.

"Wait a minute, Lam," Inspector Hobart said, as I had a hand on the knob. "How do you feel about Sellers? Did those two slaps give you hard feelings?"

I looked at him and said, "Yes."

"Going to make any difference in the way you co-operate with me?"

"No."

"Going to make you try to get even with Sellers?"

"Not the way he thinks."

Hobart grinned. "Go on. Get the hell out of here," he said.

CHAPTER NINE

IT was quarter to eleven by the time I reached Ernestine Hamilton's apartment.

She must have been waiting within six feet of the door because I had no sooner pressed the button than the door was jerked open and Ernestine all but grabbed me into her arms.

"Donald!" she exclaimed, "I'm *so* glad ... I was afraid you weren't going to show up."

"I was unavoidably detained," I told her.

There were traces of tears in her eyes.

"I know," she said. "I've been telling myself that for the last hour but ... well, I got to thinking and wondering if perhaps you hadn't handed me a line. You know, I must have seemed an awful ninny to you last night and I was afraid I'd disgusted you and ..."

"Stop it," I said.

"Stop what?"

"This business of running yourself down," I said. "From now on, you're going to think of yourself in an entirely different manner. Did you ask Bernie about——"

"I asked her about everything," she said. "I told her to tell me everything in that hotel that looked the least bit unusual. And, believe me, I turned her inside out. Donald, you'd be absolutely surprised at the things that go on in a big hotel like that.

"Of course, the house detectives know some of it, but I don't think they know as much as a good, smart telephone operator—and, of course, the house detectives don't do anything about things unless they feel that a situation is something that's apt to create a disturbance or hurt the good name of the hotel in some way, or—well, you know, give it a bad reputation.

"My gosh, Donald, we didn't get to sleep until three o'clock this morning and Bernie is so tired she can hardly hold her head up. Believe me, I got *all* the dirt. There's the married woman in 917 whose husband is away on a trip. There's a girl who slipped into another room and then found she'd left her purse with her key in it. She'd locked her purse with her key in it, her driving license, all of her money, everything, in the man's room."

"Nothing that would help on this case?" I asked.

"I couldn't find a thing. I just turned Bernie inside out about everything. It would take me an hour to tell you all of it. I made some notes and———"

"Let's go down to the hotel," I said. "Is there any chance of meeting Bernie?"

She shook her head. "Bernie's on the switchboard right straight through. She takes her lunch.

"Donald, there's one thing that might interest you and that's the unclaimed brief case."

"What about it?" I asked.

"Well, when guests come in they come in by taxi or by private car and unload their baggage out front. That's the doorman's jurisdiction. He takes the baggage and piles it by the entrance. The bell boys take it from there and put it all in a big row while they wait for the guests to register and be assigned rooms.

"After a guest is assigned a room the clerk calls out, 'Front,' and a bell boy comes and picks up the key and the clerk says, 'Take Mr. So-and-So to Room such-and-such.'

"So then the guest goes over to the row of baggage and indicates the bags that are his and the boy takes them up to the room."

"Go on," I said. "What about the unclaimed brief case?"

"Well, you know how it is, Donald, during the rush hour, along early in the morning when the planes come in. There's a lot of luggage that piles up there, quite a row of it. Then along during the slack time of day there won't be any luggage at all. Then it will build up again along in the afternoon. For some reason people don't check in quite as much during the middle of the day. Well, anyway, when they got all caught up with their baggage yesterday, there was one brief case left over. Some incoming guest had evidently failed to remember that he had a brief case and had gone up to his room and just left it sitting there."

"All right," I said, "there was an unclaimed brief case. What happened to it?"

"It was turned into the Lost and Found, but no one's claimed it."

"Let's go take a look," I said.

"You think the brief case could be important, Donald?"

"Anything could be important; anything that's the least bit out of the ordinary."

"Heavens," she said, "I never realized how many things happen that are out of the ordinary in a hotel of that sort—that is, things that I'd call out of the ordinary.

"What detained you, Donald?"

I said, "I was questioned by the police."

"*You* were?"

"That's right."

"Why?"

"Oh, they thought I might know something."

"Donald, you're so mysterious and so casual and off-hand about these things. I ... Donald, I'm so excited I'm trembling like a leaf."

"You've got to get over that," I said.

"I don't know what's got into me," she said. "Just the idea of associating with ... with a private eye.... Donald, I'm so excited I couldn't eat a bit of breakfast. I managed to drink the coffee but I just didn't want a thing to eat this morning. And poor Bernie, she's absolutely all in. The look she gave me when she left.... I just kept her awake half the night."

"Okay," I said, "let's go to the hotel."

We went to the hotel and Ernestine, who knew most of the employees, was proud as a peacock, taking me in tow and nodding to the bell boys and one of the porters. Then she took me over to the porter's office and said, "He handles the Lost and Found."

The porter looked me over, then looked at Ernestine as though he had never fully appraised her before.

Ernestine said, "John, my friend wants to see that brief case that was picked up. The sleeper that no one claimed. He——"

The porter produced the brief case.

"Locked?" I asked.

He nodded.

"That wouldn't be any handicap, would it?" I asked.

"Why?"

"I'd like to look inside of it."

"Yours?"

"It could be."

"Oh, I know John could open it," Ernestine said. "He's clever with locks, and he has all sorts of keys, don't you, John?"

The porter opened a drawer containing half a dozen key rings, selected one with small keys on it, tried a couple of keys without doing any good. On the third try the lock clicked back and the brief case opened.

I looked inside.

It was a brief case that held three compartments. There was a bloodstained knife in the middle compartment. There was a chamois-skin money belt also bloodstained, and nothing else.

The porter got a brief glimpse of the knife. He started to reach for the brief case. I grabbed his wrist.

"Don't touch it," I said. "It's been contaminated enough already. Don't touch a thing. We'll let the fingerprint men work on it."

"Oh, Donald, what is it?" Ernestine asked.

I said, "Ernestine, I'm putting you in charge. Don't let anybody or anything touch that brief case. Tie a string around the handle so we don't leave any more fingerprints or smudge any that might be on there. Now then, where's the telephone?"

The porter said, "Use this one right here and I'll listen while you're doing your talking."

I rang up police headquarters and asked for Inspector Hobart. After a few seconds I had him on the line. "Lam talking, Inspector," I said.

"Okay, Lam, what's on your mind?"

"You have found the murder weapon," I said.

"*I* have?"

"Yes, *you.*"

"Where?"

"At the hotel in a brief case."

Hobart hesitated for a moment, then said, "I don't like that, Donald."

"Why not?"

"It's too fast. It was too easy. You may be a smart investigator, but on this you're *too* damned smart."

I said, "If you and Sellers hadn't interfered with my schedule this morning I'd have had it earlier."

"You knew it was there?"

"I was looking," I said.

"Where are you now?"

"In the porter's office at the hotel."

"Don't go away," Hobart said. "Don't let anybody touch anything. I'm coming down."

"Okay," I said, and started to hang up.

"Just a minute," the porter said, and pushed me away from the telephone. "Hello," he said, "this is the porter at the hotel. With whom am I talking?"

The receiver made squawking noises.

"All right," the porter said. "I'll see that no one touches anything and that everyone stays here. You're coming right down? Okay, thanks."

The porter hung up and said apologetically to Ernestine, "I know you, Ernestine, but I don't know this man, and this is important. The police are coming right down."

Ernestine grabbed my arm. Her fingers clamped so tight they hurt.

"Donald," she squealed. "Oh, Donald, I'm so excited ... I suppose I'm going to have to learn to control myself, but this thing is ... this is terrific!"

The porter looked at her speculatively. "How did you know that knife was in there?" he asked me.

"I didn't."

"You came and asked for it." He turned to Ernestine. "Who is this guy?"

"Donald Lam," I said, "of Cool and Lam, Los Angeles."

"All right, what's Cool and Lam?"

"Investigators."

"Private eyes?"

"Call us that if you want."

"How did you know what to ask for and what to look for?"

"I didn't. I looked. I found."

"Also, you asked."

"I asked," I said.

"That's the part I want to know about."

"That's the part the police may want to know about," I said. "You can stick around and listen."

"I'll be sticking around and listening," he promised. "Don't worry."

Inspector Hobart made it in record time. He had a laboratory man with him. I showed him what we had. The laboratory man took it into custody and Hobart wanted to know about Ernestine.

I told him.

Hobart looked me over and said, "All right, let's go."

He took Ernestine and me out to the squad car and up to Headquarters.

I was back in his office within an hour and a half of the time I'd left it.

"Private investigators," Hobart said, "can serve papers and get evidence in divorce cases and things of that sort. The police solve murder cases."

I nodded.

"I just wanted to be sure you understood that," he said.

"What does that mean?" Ernestine asked.

"It means," Inspector Hobart said, "that your boy friend is inclined to take in too damn much territory."

Ernestine flushed and said hastily. "He's not my boy friend."

Hobart looked us both over. "You sit there," he said to Ernestine. He crooked his forefinger at me. "Lam, you come with me."

He took me into another room and said, "Give."

"On what?"

"Ernestine."

I said, "Ernestine is a TV enthusiast. She's nuts over private eyes."

"Go on."

"She's the roommate of Bernice Glenn, who is a telephone operator at the hotel.

"Bernice is easy on the eyes and attractive to men. She goes out. She seldom eats a meal in the apartment. Ernestine keeps the place clean and thrills to hear Bernice's adventures when she gets home at night from a date. That's Ernestine's whole life, vicarious substitution of other people's experiences for her own. She gets her romantic adventures by listening to Bernice. She gets her excitement from watching television.

"When she found out I was a private detective she looked at me with stars in her eyes."

"What are you doing, just playing her along?" I said. "Believe it or not, I've got plans for Ernestine."

"Such as what?"

"I think I'll get her a job."

"Where?"

"In Los Angeles."

"Doing what?"

"Being an operative."

"Has she had any experience?"

"She has talents."

"Keep talking."

"Notice her face," I said. 'She does her hair all wrong. She's so eager to learn about life from other people that she doesn't stop to think about living her own life herself. If she keeps on she'll be a mousy person with frustrations. If she can only learn to quit selling herself short she's going to marry some earnest, sincere guy who will make her a good husband and she'll make a wonderful wife and mother, and, later on, a damn fine grandmother."

"So what do you intend to do?"

"Get her excited, get her to break out of her shell, to take a look at life, get her doing things, get her to use some sense in the way she does her hair, get her to develop some of her natural aptitudes."

"Trying to turn a wallflower into a vamp in the approved Hollywood tradition, aren't you?" he asked.

"Don't be silly," I said. "I don't want her to be a vamp. She doesn't want to be a vamp. She loves people. She wants human contacts. She wants to feel she belongs. She doesn't want to be a sultry *femme fatale*. She wants to be an honest hard-working girl with an honest, hard-working husband. She wants to raise a family that will be a credit to her and to the community. In the meantime, she has exceptional talents of observation and dependability."

"You've just gone off your rocker falling for a dame who appealed to your sympathies," Hobart said. "It takes talent and training to be a detective. You damned amateurs! You give me a pain."

I said, "We found the murder weapon, didn't we?"

117

He looked at me, grinned, and said, "Ouch!"

After a while he took out his pack of cigarettes, gave me one, took one himself, and said, "How the hell *did* you happen to find it?"

I said, "Ernestine found it for me."

"All right, how did *she* happen to find it for you?"

"Because I asked her to look for it."

"And what brought that up?"

I said, "I wanted to find out whatever was unusual about events in the hotel. I wanted to find out what was going on. I asked her to find out everything that was the least bit out of the ordinary, reviewing all the things that had happened there in the hotel."

"Was that looking for a murder weapon?" he asked.

"Something like that," I said. "You kill a man with a carving knife. You don't carry the knife out with you."

"Why not?"

"In the first place, it's incriminating. In the second place, it's hard to carry."

"The murderer carried it *in* with him," Hobart said. "He could carry it *out* with him."

"That's what puzzles me," I said.

"What does?"

"It isn't the kind of knife that a man would carry with him as a weapon. A knife that was intended to be a weapon would be of rigid, heavy steel, with a keen edge for the blade and a heavy back. Or it might be a two-edged stiletto type of affair. This thing is a carving knife. It has a peculiar onyx handle."

"How do you know?"

"I saw that much when I looked in the brief case."

Hobart's eyes narrowed. "Right. What else do you know?"

I said, "I don't think the murderer carried the knife in with him. I think that knife originally came from someplace in the hotel. I think someone must have had access to the kitchen or to room service—unless the knife was bought at some store near the hotel by someone who suddenly decided it would be nice to have a weapon.

"If you hadn't interfered with my activities I'd have been scouting around the neighbourhood, talking with hardware stores."

"Then it's a damn good thing we interfered with your activities," Hobart said. "That's the trouble with you amateurs. You underestimate the intelligence of the police. I've had men out covering the hardware and cutlery stores for the past fifteen minutes. We should get a report soon.

"For your information, Lam, that is a peculiar knife. This imitation onyx handle is a species of plastic that is relatively new. The knife comes from Chicago. We telephoned the distributor to find out how many wholesalers here had carried it.

"There's just one jobber on the Coast that put in an order and his shipment just came in a few days ago. A few of the salesmen had samples but that's all. They haven't made any retail deliveries."

"Then this knife came from the stock of the wholesaler?"

Hobart shook his head. "I don't know. *We* can't afford to jump at conclusions. We're making a canvass right now on each one of their salesmen. The jobber is asking them to report on whether they can return the samples to stock. That way they can tell if one knife is missing. Apparently the rest of the shipment is intact.

"The plastic on the knife handle is a new type. The design is new, and the blade is a new type of steel that is designed to hold its edge almost indefinitely. The knife is exceptionally thin. This new steel that has only been on the market a short time comes from Sweden."

"That should make the knife easy to trace," I said.

Hobart nodded and said, "If one salesman doesn't have his sample we'll find out what he did with it and start tracing the murder weapon from there. That's the kind of a break we don't ordinarily get in a murder case."

"So what do I do?" I asked.

"You wait," he said. "You do absolutely nothing. I don't want you going out and gumming up the works. This is a job for a Police Department, a whole department, you understand. One lone guy prowling around and asking questions can do more harm than good.

"Now then, I want some cards face up on the table. You weren't interested in solving a murder. You were up here on something else. What?"

I looked him in the eye and said, "Fifty grand."

"That's better," he said. "I thought so. What were you planning to do?"

"Turn it in for a reward," I said.

"Sellers wouldn't like that. He wants to solve the case himself."

"Let him solve it then. I'm not stopping him. He's got the whole damned Police Department back of him. He can do more than I can."

Hobart looked at me and said, "You can't get along in your business if you have police enmity."

"I won't have anyone's enmity after I've got the fifty grand," I said. "Sure, Sellers would *like* to solve it, but what he absolutely *needs* is to have it proved that someone else had the fifty grand. Once he does that, he's clean.

"I'll tell you something else. If we get a reward we're willing to let Sellers take all the credit."

Hobart drummed with his fingers on the desk. "Lam," he said, "I'm going to ask you something. You don't need to answer it if you don't want to, but don't lie to me. We're working on a case where false information could cross us up more than anything else."

I nodded.

"Did you have that fifty grand?"

"Would you protect me?" I asked.

"It depends. I'm not making any promises."

I said, "Yes."

"Yes, what?"

"Yes, I had the fifty grand."

"Then that story you fed Frank Sellers about this man, Inman, at the Full Dinner Pail having it was just a cock-and-bull story?"

"That wasn't a cock-and-bull story," I said. "I think Inman had it before I did."

Hobart's eyes narrowed. "All right," he said. "Where did you get it?"

"I got it from Downer's trunk."

"And where did you get Downer's trunk?"

"I picked it up at the railroad station."

"Where is it now?"

I told him.

"Go on," he said. "What happened to the fifty grand?"

I said, "Either one of two people have it."

"Who?"

"Either Takahashi Kisarazu, who runs the camera store, or Evelyn Ellis."

"What's your reasoning?"

I said, "I bought a camera and some enlarging paper. I took some paper out of the box of enlarging paper. I don't know how many sheets, probably fifteen or twenty. The camera store says they found seventeen sheets of paper under the counter so I'll settle for seventeen."

"And you put the money in there with the rest of the enlarging paper and closed the box?"

I nodded.

"How do you know the money wasn't taken out in Los Angeles?"

"It was done by somebody in a camera store," I said.

"How do you know?"

"Because when Sellers got into the package in Los Angeles the box of enlarging paper had the seals cut all right so I wouldn't be suspicious, but it was a *different box of paper*. It was a *full* box. If it had been my box, seventeen sheets would have been missing."

Hobart said, "All right, Lam, I think you're coming clean. I'll tell you what I'll do. I'll do some work on that Jap at the camera store."

I shook my head.

"No?" he asked.

"No."

"Why not?"

"I'm not sure," I said. "I want to be sure."

"How are you going to be sure?"

"I don't know, but I have an idea the murder of Downer was tied in with the loss of fifty grand."

"The murder is my meat," Hobart said.

"You can have it. I want the money. You keep your meat. I'll keep mine."

"All right. What do *you* think happened?"

I said, "I think that Baxley had a partner in the Full Dinner Pail Drive-in. I think Baxley didn't know the police were after him until after he'd made that telephone call and looked back over his shoulder. I think Baxley went to that drive-in and ordered the two hamburgers, one with onions and one without onions, so he'd have a good excuse to have them put in a paper sack. Then I think he sat there and ate the hamburgers slowly and leisurely so people could see him eating the hamburgers. I think that was all part of the plan. Then I think he took the fifty grand, which was the split of his partner, put it in the paper bag, threw the paper bag into the refuse can and drove off.

"I think that's where Sellers made his first mistake. I think he should have pulled back the lid on that trash can and pulled out that paper bag. *Then* I think he should have tagged along after Baxley."

"Then where did Downer get the fifty grand?"

"He got it from Baxley's accomplice," I said, "and because there wasn't any split, it means that he had to high-jack it. If he'd shown up with twenty-five grand I'd have figured there were three partners in the job, that Baxley got half and the other two split another half for setting the thing up for him. Because Downer had fifty grand, it means it was a highjack."

Inspector Hobart said, "I've got news for you, Lam."

"What?"

"It didn't work out that way and it isn't going to be that way when we get the thing unscrambled."

"Why?"

"I don't know," Hobart said. "Call it a cop's instinct if you want, but things don't come out that smooth. You've got a bright idea and that's all it is, an idea.

"That's the worst of you guys who single-shot. You play things as a lone wolf. You get an idea and you follow it through. You work out some ingenious solution and then you start playing that solution. The cops can't afford to work that way. They had to go one step at a time. They can't take short cuts. They plod along, picking out one thing and then another."

"Okay. You work your way, I work my way," I said.

"What else do you know?" Hobart asked.

I said, "There were things in that trunk that I couldn't figure out—cords, books and things. Sellers has them now."

Hobart said, "Tell me about these cards."

"They consisted of strings of figures." I pulled out my notebook. "Here's one—O, O, five, one, three, six, four."

Hobart reached out and took the book.

"Now then, take a look at the next one," I said.

Hobart read out the figures. "Four, dash, five, dash, fifty-nine, dash, ten, dash, one, dash."

"Take a look at the next line," I said. "That ends in a plus sign."

He read off the figures. "Eight, dash, five, dash, fifty-nine, dash, one, with a plus at the end of it.

"Try one of your hunches on this stuff," Hobart suggested.

I said, "I noticed a lot of the numbers on those cards ended with three, six, four."

"Any ideas?"

"I've been thinking, particularly about that plus and minus."

"All right, Lam," he said. "I'm going to let you think some more. You're going to sit right here."

"What about Ernestine?" I asked.

"I'm going to let the matron keep her in charge for a little while."

"You're holding her?"

"Not exactly holding her," Hobart said, "but I want to get this damn case buttoned up, and I can't do it if I've got a lot of temperamental prima donnas running around the city playing hunches. If that damned Jap is mixed in this thing I want to shake him down."

I said, "You keep out of my end of it and I'll keep out of yours."

He grinned and said, "You'll damn well keep out of everything. You won't be in circulation. You don't have any end."

He strode out of the place and closed the door behind him.

I sat there for a long while. There wasn't anything else to do. I studied the copies of the cards that had been in the trunk.

After a while the door opened and an officer came in with a couple of hamburgers wrapped in paper napkins and a carton of milk.

"Compliments of Inspector Hobart," he said.

"Where is he?"

"Working."

"I want to see him."

"So do lots of other people."

"I may have something he'd like to know about," I said.

"He wouldn't like that."

"Why not?"

"You were supposed to tell him all you knew the first time."

"Tell him I've thought of something."

The man nodded and went out.

I finished the hamburgers, drank the milk, put the empty carton in the paper bag and dropped them in the wastebasket.

Fifteen minutes later Inspector Hobart came in. He looked flushed and angry.

"All right," he snapped. "What the hell have you been holding out?"

"Nothing. I have another idea. I've been thinking about those figures."

He made a gesture of irritation, started to go out, then said, "All right. Give it to me fast. I'll listen."

I said, "A lot of those figures end in three, six, four. Now suppose those were telephone numbers written backwards."

"What do you mean?"

"Three, six, four," I said, "would be H, O, three. Then the numbers on this first card would be Hollywood three, one, five hundred. That would be a telephone number. Now then, if you found that the man at that number made a bet on the fourth of May, nineteen hundred fifty-nine, at ten to one and lost, and then on eighth of May, made a bet at four to one, and won, it might explain something."

Hobart paused for a minute, came back to the table, drew up a chair, reached for my notebook and started studying the figures. After a while he said, "It's an idea. For your information, we've got the original books and the original cards. I'm going to start checking them on that theory."

"What else do you know?" I asked.

"Lots," he said, and got up and walked out.

An hour and a half later Hobart was back again. "Lam," he said, "you have hunches. Some of them are damn good hunches. I hate to say so because I tell my men not to play hunches. I tell them to go one step at a time, not to get brilliant, just keep methodical."

I nodded.

"However," he said, "for your information, the guy at Hollywood three, one, five hundred had been playing the races but not with Downer. He'd made a bet on a horse at ten to one odds on the fourth of May and had lost. He made a bet on the eighth of May at four to one odds and had won. We've run down a couple of other cards and they check out.

"Now then, this is your hunch. What does it mean?"

"I don't know," I said. "I hesitate to try to parlay that information into a winning combination but if you want another hunch I'll give you one."

"What's that?"

I said, "This shipment of thousand-dollar bills that was stolen, that's kind of a peculiar shipment—a hundred thousand in thousand-dollar bills."

"Go on," he said.

I said, "It must have been a special order. The bank that ordered that shipment of one hundred thousand in thousand dollar bills just might have had Standley Downer as a depositor and it might have been Standley Downer who ordered the hundred grand in thousand-dollar bills."

"Why?"

"Because he was intending to liquidate and get out," I said, "and he wanted the dough to carry with him."

"And then?" Hobart asked.

"Then," I said, "somebody who knew Downer knew that he had ordered the hundred grand and decided to highjack the dough. But if this person knew Downer, then Downer knew this person. So we may have a sort of ring-around-the-rosy. And this person also had to know what armored truck would be making the shipment."

"Now, that is something I won't buy," Hobart said. "That's the worst of you brilliant guys. You get one good hunch that pays off and it paves the way for playing a thousand hunches that don't.

"I'm sorry I listened to you the first time. I find myself trying to play short cuts. That's a hell of a way to solve crimes. That's the way they solve 'em on television, where they have only half an hour in which to show the crime, bring the solution and drag in a half-dozen commercials, all in thirty little minutes. Count 'em, thirty.

"You go to hell. You're corrupting me. I won't watch television for fear my thinking will be contaminated. You're corrupting me worse than television."

He got up and walked out.

Ten minutes later he was back.

"I can't get you out of my mind," he said. "You've ruined my method of approach."

He handed me the copy of *Hardware Age* that I'd picked up in Evelyn Ellis' apartment.

"Ernestine said that you had this magazine with you when you came up to her apartment last night. When you left you forgot to take it with you."

"And so?" I asked.

"What were you doing with a copy of *Hardware Age*? Why did you want it?"

"I just wanted to read it."

"It's an old copy. Where did you get it?"

I said, "I got it from Evelyn Ellis' room in the hotel. I was reading it when she decided to get rough and get me out of there."

"And you went?"

"I went."

"Why the abrupt departure?"

"Because she was tearing her clothes off and was going to yell assault with intent to commit rape when she had 'em all off—and she didn't have far to go."

"Then the magazine is hers?"

"I guess so."

"What would she be doing with it?"

I said, "If you look through it you'll probably find a photograph of Evelyn in a bathing suit as Miss Hardware. She was chosen as the queen of the hardware convention."

Hobart snapped his fingers and said, "There you go. Another example of what happens when you get away from steady, plodding detective work."

"Why?"

"I turned every page of that damn thing from cover to cover," he said, "trying to find her picture. It isn't there.

"That's what comes of playing hunches. You and television will be the ruination of a lot of good cops."

He was so mad he slammed the magazine down on the table and started to leave the room. He was within two feet of the door when it was opened by an officer who handed him a message typewritten on a piece of paper.

"Thought you might like to see this, Inspector," he said.

Hobart looked at the message, frowned, looked at it again, said, "They're sure?"

The officer nodded.

Hobart said, "All right. I'll take it from here."

He folded the message, shoved it down in his pocket and stood thoughtfully looking at the door as it closed behind the departing officer.

"All right," he said, turning to me, "here's a puzzle for you. You like to be brilliant. Go ahead and be brilliant on this one."

"What is it?" I asked.

"The outfit that makes this knife hasn't sold a single carving knife any place west of Denver except that one San Francisco shipment. They're developing the territory regionally.

"Colfax and Bristol, the hardware jobbers here who saw the knife at the hardware convention, insisted on having the first shipment to the Coast, backing it up with a definite order. They got their shipment four days ago.

"Now then, every one of their salesmen has been checked and each man reports that he has his sample intact."

"Well," I said, "what would *you* do if you'd committed a murder with a knife, ditched the weapon and then somebody contacted you on the telephone and asked to report whether or not you had the knife—what would you say?"

"Oh, sure," Hobart said, "that occurred to me a long time ago. We're going to have to have men check every one of those salesmen. But somehow I have an idea they'll check out, and that will leave us right back where we started."

He went out of the room. Because there was nothing else to do, I picked up the hardware magazine and started reading it from cover to cover.

Suddenly I found an item that made sense. I kicked myself for not having thought of it and went to the door and jerked it open.

A uniformed officer was sitting outside the door in a straight-backed chair tilted back against the wall, his heels braced on a cross-rung. As I opened the door he snapped forward so that the other two legs of the chair came down on the floor with a bang and his bulk came up out of the chair, "No, you don't, brother," he said. "You stay right there."

"All right, I stay here," I said, "but get me Inspector Hobart. I have to see him."

"Well, *that's* something," the officer said. "You're running the place now?"

I said, "You get Inspector Hobart or you're both going to be sorry," stepped back inside the room and closed the door.

Ten minutes later Inspector Hobart came pushing into the room. "Now this," he said, "has damn well got to be good. If it isn't good, you'll do your waiting in a cell."

"I think it's good," I said.

"Let's hope so. What is it, another brainy idea of flashing brilliance?"

I said, "An article in the *Hardware Age*. Want me to read it?"

"What's it about?"

"Just a paragraph of news comments about the convention in New Orleans."

"What does it say?"

I picked it up and read: "Christopher, Crowder and Doyle Cutlery Company of Chicago announced a new general utility carving knife which will be placed on the market first in the eastern territory and then in the western territory. A distinguishing feature of the knife is the resilient toughness of the steel which makes it possible to use an exceedingly thin blade. President Carl Christopher points out the blade is almost as thin as a sheet of paper. A new synthetic makes the plastic handle look like onyx.

"Evelyn Ellis, Miss American Hardware, presented carving sets to some hundred buyers who were asked to drop by the booth of the Christopher, Crowder and Doyle Cutlery

Company between four and five in the afternoon and receive complimentary carving sets in plush-lined boxes."

I folded the magazine back so it was open at the page from which I had been reading and handed it to Inspector Hobart.

He didn't look at the magazine, but instead looked me over and said, "Somehow I can appreciate the way Frank Sellers feels."

"What do you mean?"

"I regard you with mingled emotions," Hobart said. "I'm not going to pretend that this isn't an important lead. It's one I should have thought of myself. Of course, this babe had one of those carving sets. After all, she was the queen of the hardware industry. She was taken to New Orleans and paraded around in evening gowns and bathing suits. She had all of her expenses paid, was given a big build-up and a lot of publicity.

"She must have picked up a lot of loot, and if she was giving away carving sets to buyers who stopped by the booth during the time the company was announcing its new number, it's a cinch she picked up a carving set for herself. Now, all we've got to do is to get a search warrant, go through the hotel, find the box containing the fork that matches this knife and ask her where the hell the knife is and see what she says.

"That's fine. I'm grateful. But you do these things too damned easy and there's just a little too much of a flourish about the way you wrap these things up. Oh, hell, Lam, I suppose I'm nervous, irritable and upset. I'm in my office on the telephone flashing messages out to the dispatcher, getting reports, trying to cover the whole damn front and you sit in here with nothing to do except sharp-shoot. No wonder you can high-grade the stuff. But it makes me just a little mad."

"At me?" I asked, trying to look innocent.

"You're damn right, at you," he said. "But half at myself. I should have thought of this myself. It's the way the breaks come. I shut you in here in this damn room with nothing to look at except four walls and a hardware magazine. Naturally you read the hardware magazine. Then you come up with a lead and have all the smug modesty of a guy who's just caught a forward pass and carried it forty yards for a touchdown."

I said, with all the synthetic bitterness I could put in my voice, "That's what comes of trying to co-operate! What I *should* have done was to have kept this information to myself, chucked the hardware magazine in the wastebasket, then gone out and followed up the lead."

"There are just two things wrong with that," Hobart told me. "In fact, three things. The first one is that you aren't going out, the second one is you aren't going to follow up any leads, and the third is that any time you stumble onto something hot like this and try to hold it from me, you're going to find yourself behind the eight ball."

He stood looking at me angrily and then suddenly threw back his head and laughed. "All right, Lam," he said, "I can see it from your viewpoint. You can't see it from mine because you don't know the thousand and one things I've got to try to co-ordinate in order to put across this investigation. Anyhow, thanks for the lead. We'll follow it up."

"What's happened to Ernestine?" I asked.

"We've been pumping her to find out if *she* knows anything else that she hasn't told."

"When are you going to let us go?"

"When we get done with this phase of our investigation," he said. "We don't want you amateurs going out and lousing it up for us."

I said, "In other words, you're going to wait until you get damn good and ready to let me go and that won't be until Frank Sellers telephones from Los Angeles that it's all right to let me out of quarantine."

He smiled.

"In that case," I told him, "I demand to see a lawyer."

He shook his head. "My ears aren't good, Lam. You're talking into my bum ear."

"Turn around," I said, "so I can talk to the other one."

He just grinned, said, "Sit here and do some more thinking, Lam. Don't bother me unless you get something good. But if you get something good and don't let me know, I'll clobber you."

He took the hardware magazine with him and walked out.

CHAPTER TEN

IT was four o'clock in the afternoon when Hobart came back. "All right, Lam, we're letting you go."

"Where's Ernestine?"

"I sent her home an hour ago."

"You could have let me escort her home," I said.

He grinned. "I could have but I didn't. I let the plain-clothes officer who had been interrogating her this afternoon take her home. She was thrilled to death. She says television is tame compared with real life—how's that for a thrill?"

"All right," I said. "What plans have you got for me?"

"What plans have *you* got for you?" he asked.

"It depends on what I can do."

"I don't want you tossing monkey wrenches in the machinery. If you do, you're going to get picked up."

"How about Evelyn Ellis? Did you find the rest of the carving set?"

He said, "Don't be silly. Things only work out that easy for you gifted amateurs. For your information, Evelyn says she gave out sets containing these new knives to all of the accredited buyers who stopped by the booth of Christopher, Crowder and Doyle. She says she didn't take one for herself, that she wasn't housekeeping at the time, and wanted to know how we felt a young woman of her dimensions could conceal a carving set in a bathing suit."

"She could have wrapped it up and carried it out under her arm," I said. "She had a purse, didn't she?"

"I know," Hobart said. "We're investigating all that. Don't worry, Lam. You don't need to tell us how to investigate a homicide. You wanted to know what we found and I told you what we found—nothing."

"I can't talk with Evelyn Ellis?"

Hobart's face got hard. "Listen, Lam," he said, "get this and get it straight. You're in San Francisco. You can go to a hotel. You can go to a show. You can go to a restaurant. You can pick up a jane. You can have a good time. You can get drunk. But if you go near the Happy Daze Camera

Company, if you try to call on Evelyn Ellis, or if you hang around that hotel where the murder was committed, you're going to be thrown into the cooler. And, so help me, you'll stay there until we get this thing lined up."

"Did it ever occur to you," I said, "that I'm working on a job? That I have a responsibility to a client? That someone has highjacked me out of fifty grand and——"

"Everything has occurred to me," Hobart said wearily. "Everything has occurred to me fifty or sixty times and it keeps occurring to me. I'm trying to unscramble a mess. I don't want your fine Italian hand lousing it up."

"Can I go back to Los Angeles?"

"You can, but it wouldn't be advisable. Sellers isn't in a particularly jovial mood."

I said, "There's a Hazel Clune or a Hazel Downer that——"

"We know all about her," Hobart said. "We've had her under surveillance. She was up here the night before the murder. She's up here now."

"Now?"

He nodded.

"Where."

He started to shake his head. Then suddenly his eyes narrowed. I could see him toying with an idea. "Why do you want to know?" he asked.

"I'm doing a job for her. I can't conscientiously charge her per diem while I'm sitting on my fanny in an interrogation room in San Francisco Headquarters."

"What would you rather do, sleep in a cell or in a hotel?" Hobart asked. "Because I've changed my mind about leaving you free to run around."

"Is that a gag?"

"It's a question."

"The answer," I said, "will probably surprise you. I prefer to sleep in a hotel."

"I think it can be arranged," Hobart said, "but you'll have to co-operate."

"What do you mean, co-operate?"

"We'll get you a room in a hotel. There will be a telephone in that room but you're not going to use it for any outside calls. There's a good restaurant in the hotel with

132

room service and you can order anything sent up that you want to eat. We'll have the newspapers in there and some magazines. You can read. There'll be a television in there. You can watch television. You can go to bed. You can't try to leave the place because we'll know it if you do, and that would be too bad—for you."

"You mean I'll be in custody?"

"Not exactly. You'll be in the charge of police. You'll be left on your own, but you won't be free to leave without permission."

"How long do I have to stay there?"

"All night tonight, at least. Perhaps we can let you go in the morning."

"My partner will be worried about me."

"Your partner is worried sick about you," Hobart said. "Your office has been frantically trying to get you every place they could possibly think of. They've even called here at Headquarters."

"What did you tell them?"

"We told them we weren't holding any Donald Lam for anything. We aren't."

"You *are* holding me."

"But not for any particular charge. We're just holding you because you want to co-operate with us."

"Ernestine is going to be worrying about me," I said.

"Ernestine is on Cloud Nine," Hobart said. "She's co-operating with the police now and the plain-clothes man who's up there in the apartment with her, keeping an eye on things, is a fairly good-looking bachelor who has come to the conclusion she's a pretty sensible, level-headed sort of girl. In fact, they're rather hitting it off. I wouldn't be surprised if he isn't beating your time, Lam. What's more, he's available and you're not."

"Where is this hotel?" I asked.

"The Ocean Beach," he said. "Want to stay there or here?"

"There."

"Okay. I'll arrange it. It'll take about half an hour."

He went out, and at the end of half an hour a plain-clothes man opened the door, said, "Come on, Lam."

I followed him out to a police car. The officer drove

slowly and carefully to the Ocean Beach Hotel, which was way out on the waterfront far removed from the scene of the murder and miles from the Happy Daze Camera Company.

The officer escorted me up to the room. It was a nice, airy room.

"What are the restrictions," I asked, "about going out?"

"You don't go out."

"What about a razor, toothbrush and———"

"Your bag is over there in the corner. You'll get excellent reception on that television. There are the late papers on the table. There are only two ways out of here, the front door and the fire escape. We'll be watching the front door. Nobody will be watching the fire escape."

"How come?"

"Well," he said, "it might be cold and disagreeable sitting out there and watching the fire escape and, frankly, I think the Inspector would rather like to have you go down the fire escape."

"Why?" I asked.

"Well," he said, grinning, "it would make the case look better."

"What case?"

"The case against you."

"I didn't know there was any."

"There isn't any now, but all we need is just a little more evidence in order to have a peach of a case."

"I see," I said. "The Inspector would like to have resort to flight. Is that it?"

"Well, if you resorted to flight," the officer said, "we'd certainly have enough to hold you on a murder case. In this state, flight is an evidence of guilt—that is, it can be used in support of a prosecutor's case."

"Well," I said, "it's certainly nice of you to have told me."

"Oh, that's part of my instructions," the officer said cheerfully. "We want to be sure that if you dust out of here there's no question about it being flight. You see, I can testify now that I told you."

"Thanks a lot," I told him.

"The door won't be locked," he said. "You can bolt it

from the inside if you're nervous, but the fire escape is at the end of the hall."

"I can't go out the front door."

"That'll be guarded," he said.

"Well, I'm glad to know all the rules," I told him. "I at least have the dimensions of the trap."

"The trap?" he asked.

"Sure," I said. "Inspector Hobart would give his eye teeth to have me go down the fire escape and resort to flight. He'd love it."

"He probably would at that," the officer said, and went out.

I called room service, asked for a double manhattan cocktail, a filet mignon, rare, a baked potato, coffee and apple pie.

I was told that everything would be sent up except the cocktail. Orders were to send up no liquor.

I turned on the television and saw the last twenty minutes of a private-eye program. Then there was news and the weather forecast. After that, the meal came up. I finished the food, phoned for the waiter to take away the dishes and glanced through the newspapers.

There was a little stuff about the case of a man having been murdered in a downtown hotel, but just the usual follow-ups: The police were working on "hot leads" and expected to have a suspect in custody "within another forty-eight hours."

It was all running according to the regular pattern—the reporters having to make a story, the police having to keep the taxpayers satisfied they were on the job.

It was well after dark when I heard surreptitious knuckles tapping on the door.

I crossed the room and opened the door. Hazel Downer stood on the threshold.

"Donald!" she exclaimed.

"Well, what do you know?" I said. "It's a small world. Come on in and park the curves. How did you find me here?"

"I followed you."

"How come?"

"We found that you were being held by the police. My

attorney, Madison Ashby, called up from Los Angeles and said he was going to get a habeas corpus unless you were released. They promised him they'd release you within an hour and take you to a hotel."

"So then what?"

"I was up in San Francisco keeping in touch with him. He called me and told me, so I went down and parked in front of Headquarters. When the plainclothes officer drove you out here I followed."

"And then?"

"I didn't want to be ostentatious about it, so I waited for a couple of hours, then went and parked my car, got a taxicab, loaded some baggage in the taxicab, came up here just as bold as you please and sailed past the plainclothes man who's on duty downstairs, registered, and got a room."

"Use your right name to register under?"

"Of course not."

"You were taking a chance on being recognized."

"I don't think so. They don't know me up here."

I said, "Well, well, what do you know! So you're here in the hotel."

"That's right."

"Well, I'm sure glad to see you. I was afraid I was going to have a lonely evening."

"What do we do now, Donald?"

"What would you like to do?" I asked.

"I'd like to find out what happened to the money Standley had—the money of mine."

"What do you think happened to it?"

"I think that Evelyn Ellis got it, but I'm beginning to get all mixed up."

I grabbed a pad of paper and wrote, "The room is bugged. Follow my lead."

I shoved that in under her eyes and she laughed throatily and said, "Well, Donald, after all, you've been doing a lot of very difficult work for me and I thought it would be a good thing if we sort of brought each other up to date."

"Well, let's sit down," I said, "and I'll see if I can get a drink ... oh, dammit! I can't get a drink. They won't serve me anything alcoholic."

"Why? Do they think you're a minor?"

I said, "I'm being more or less held in protective custody."

"What happened, Donald?" she asked.

"Well, let me think," I said. "I'll have to kind of figure things out. Sit down over there. I've got to powder my nose. I'll be right with you."

She sat on the davenport. I put my finger to my lips and sat down beside her. I took the pad and wrote: "Follow my lead. Tell me all the wild-eyed stories you want, but don't tell me anything you don't want the police to know. They probably have about three separate bugs in this room. I'm going to tell you facts, but be careful what you say in reply. Don't ask me specific questions because I may not be in a position to answer."

After she had read the note I tore it up, tiptoed over to the bathroom door, flushed the note down the toilet, rattled the knob of the door, came back and said, "Well, it sure is nice to see you. I was looking forward to a lonely evening— that is, I anticipated a lonely evening. I wasn't looking forward to it with any enthusiasm."

"Can you tell me what happened, Donald?"

"Sure," I said. "I'm not going to tell you all of it because I have some things I want to keep in the background, but here's generally what happened: I came up here looking around to try and find your lost love for you, and, of couse, by the time I really got into the game he had been murdered and I was scrambling around trying to find out something about the murder.

"Now, I'm not particularly interested in the murder because I know you're interested in the fifty thousand. Tell me, Hazel, were you fond of him?"

"Sure I was fond of him," she said. And then added, "I've been fond of lots of people. When a person has fifty grand it is easier to be fond of him."

"You're sure he had it?"

"Oh, yes. He was loaded with money."

"But you're sure he had fifty grand?"

"Well, he had quite a slug of money, Donald. He promised me sixty thousand."

"He promised you?"

"Yes, he was going to give it to me as sort of a nest egg."

"And then what happened?"

"Well, you know what happened. He began to start talking about doing this and doing that and doing the other, and getting more and more vague about what he was going to do with me. Well, it wasn't very long before I found out about that Evelyn Ellis. You know, a woman has ways of finding out those things. I guess there's something intuitive in our makeup."

"And then?" I asked.

"Well, Donald, if you want me to tell you the whole truth, I made a big mistake. I didn't play my cards right. In place of just getting in and beating that other woman's time, I made a fool of myself."

"What did you do?"

"Oh, I accused him of cheating on me and made a scene and all the things that it comes easy for a woman to do under circumstances like that, but which actually are the last things in the world she should do."

"Then what?"

"Well, then I knew he was getting ready to skip out. I thought he'd leave me fairly well provided for, but the beast just walked out without leaving me anything. That's why I got you to try and find him. If you could have found him I'd have got money out of him."

"How much?"

"I don't know. I told you he'd talked sixty grand to make it look big, but that's only a figure. I probably would have got fifteen or twenty thousand. You see, I was using you and your partner in sort of a come-on. I'm afraid I'm not very honest, Donald."

"How would you have gone about making him come through?"

"I know too much about him."

I closed one eye in a wink and said, "Now, listen, Hazel, I want to get this straight. Is there *any* chance that he was mixed up in that robbery of the armored truck?"

"I don't think so, Donald. I don't think there's a whisper of a chance."

"Tell me the truth. *Did* you know Baxley?"

"He called up once or twice. I don't know how he got my number."

"You have never had any dates with him?"

"Heavens, no."

"You told me you said yes to Standley in front of an altar. Was that true?"

"No."

"You never married him?"

"I said yes to him, but it was an automobile, not in front of an altar."

I wrote on the pad: "Keep talking. Never mind what you say. Keep talking."

She looked at me speculatively and went on, "I suppose you think I'm something of a tramp and I guess perhaps I am. I don't suppose you have any idea what it means to a girl to realize that she's forfeited her right to the one thing a woman really needs, and that's security.

"Then Standley came along. He was good to me and the guy was loaded with money. I don't know where he was making it, but I have a pretty good idea. He was in partnership with someone and they were running a betting service. He fell for me like a ton of bricks. He was going to do a lot for me—he said. He gave me quite a bit of money and I thought there was going to be lots more where that came from. He kept promising me complete financial security. He said he was going to make a settlement on me of sixty thousand dollars."

"Fifty or sixty?" I asked.

"Sixty," she said.

I said, "Keep talking."

All the time she was talking I was writing. I wrote a message:

They can hear everything we say. They're probably making tape recordings. I have to leave here. That's the thing they'd like to have me do because then they would claim it was flight and evidence of guilt. Now, what I want you to do is to pretend that you're leaving, but *I'll* be the one that leaves. I'll close the door and you can depend it's you going out. Say good-by to me and all that stuff. Then *you* come back and start making sounds. Turn on the television. Leave it on for a while but change stations every so often so that they can hear there

139

is someone in the room. Flush the toilet. Cough—but of course don't let them hear your voice. You'll have to sit up until midnight and keep the television going, changing stations once in a while. Then, if I'm not back, go to bed. From time to time, wake up and cough. Leave the door unlocked so I can get in. Can you do this? I think I can help you if you do it, and I know one thing for sure—you can help me.

She read the note and kept right on with her talking, saying, "Donald, I think you've been perfectly wonderful. I don't know why it is that a woman will take a look at some man and feel she can trust him. I guess sometimes it's a bad way to feel because you get hooked, but I feel I can trust you. I'd do anything for you, anything at all."

She backed up her statement by nodding her head.

"You don't think," I said, "there was any chance that Standley was in partnership with Baxley and that they robbed that——"

"Don't be silly, Donald," she interrupted. "Standley wasn't that kind of a man at all. He was a gambler, and, frankly, Donald, I think he was some sort of a con man. I don't know. He had some way of making money and it just rolled in. I've never seen a man who was as loaded with money as Standley Downer.

"I liked him. At first, I guess I was in love with him and I probably would have stayed in love with him if it hadn't been for the way he acted with Evelyn.

"However, I came to know him pretty well after we'd had our so-called marriage. Standley was restless. He was a man who was never satisfied with anything except motion and change. He had to be going from one thing to another just as fast as he could. He could never settle down. He couldn't settle down with anyone.

"What makes me mad about Evelyn is that she was just a gold digger. Oh, I know ... I'm not supposed to be anything but a gold digger myself. But I can tell you, Donald, that's been my trouble. I haven't looked out for Number One enough. I've always gone along with some guy and ... well, that's the way it is—that's the way I am."

"How many guys have you gone along with?" I asked.

"Too many," she said. "Not many in one way, but too many in another. No one's going to come along and propose marriage to me and expect me to wear a white bridal veil walking down to the altar. No one's going to propose marriage to me, period. I've been a kept woman and kept women can't quit."

"I can understand how you felt about Standley," I said.

"I knew you could, Donald. You're understanding."

I nodded my head and pointed to the door.

"Well, Donald," she said, "I've got to go. I just had to see you, I wanted to talk with you and ... I don't know, Donald. I want *you* to understand *me*.

"Now, I've got to go down to my room and write some letters and then get some beauty sleep. Will I see you in the morning?"

"Why not?" I asked. "How about breakfast?"

"Donald, I just want you to know how much I appreciate your loyalty and devotion and ... and I'm going to kiss you good night."

We went to the door. I opened the door. She said, "Good night, Donald."

I said speculatively, "Do you have to go, Hazel?"

She laughed throatily and said, "Of course I have to go, Donald. I'm ... well, I'm indiscreet, but I'm *not* a tramp. Anything with you would be just casual. I'm not casual, I'm ... oh, I don't know. See you for breakfast, Donald. Good night."

She kissed me. It was quite a kiss.

I walked out and closed the door, took the key Hazel had given me, went down to her room; then, after a while, went out to the fire escape and looked out.

Everything seemed to be clear.

The fire escape was one of those iron stairway affairs that zigzagged down the side of the building. The bottom segment was on a powerful spring which held the iron ladder high enough so it couldn't be reached from the ground. However, when a person descended the ladder, the weight of his body caused the last section of the ladder to lower.

I prowled around the hallway until I located a utility closet. It was locked but a celluloid pocket calendar about the size of a business card furnished a flexible medium which could be wormed in the crack of the door and was firm enough to push back the latch on the spring lock.

I looked around inside among the odds and ends in the closet and finally found a small coil of rope.

I went back to the fire escape, reconnoitred once more, crawled out on the fire escape, walked down the iron stairway until I came to the last section.

I felt my way cautiously down the last leg of the fire escape. Under my weight the metallic stairway slowly descended.

I knew I was being a sucker. I knew that the one thing the police wanted was to have me resort to flight. However, I had no alternative if I was going to stand a whisper of a chance of getting my hands on that fifty grand that I'd lost.

On the last step of the fire escape I passed the rope around the iron tread, tied it in a knot, then jumped down to the ground. Relieved of my weight, the spring in the iron stairway moved it smoothly back up to a point some fifteen feet off the ground.

The rope was a little short but by jumping up I could catch hold of the end.

I walked around the back of the hotel through an alley, stayed with the alley for two blocks, came out on a street which led to the beach. It was ten or fifteen minutes before I picked up a cruising taxicab.

I sent the cab driver toward town, telling him I'd have to give him the destination by sight because I couldn't remember the street address.

Halfway to town I had him stop at a phone booth. I called Ernestine's apartment.

A feminine voice answered.

"Ernestine?" I asked.

"Just a moment. I'll call her."

I figured that was either Bernice or a policewoman who had been assigned to stay with Ernestine.

A few moments later, Ernestine's voice, sounding rather cautious, said, "Hello."

"Don't mention any names, Ernestine," I said. "Are you alone?"

"No."

"I know Bernice is there. Is there an officer there?"

"No, just Bernice and I."

"This is Donald," I said. "I want to see you."

"Donald!" she exclaimed. 'Oh, Donald, I do so want to see you! Can you come up?"

"I'm coming up," I said.

"Oh, Donald, I have so much to tell you. Oh, it's been such an exciting day! Such a simply wonderful, wonderful——"

"Save it," I said. "I don't know whether your phone is bugged or not. If it is, you won't see me because they'll have me in custody the minute I step out of the taxicab. If I get as far as your room I'm probably all right. Be ready to open the door as soon as you hear my knock, and, if possible, I'd like to talk with Bernice as well as you."

"Oh, Bernie is terribly thrilled. She——"

"Save it," I told her, "until I get there."

I hung up, got back to the taxicab and didn't seem too positive of where I wanted to go. "It's an apartment house somewhere," I said. "I'll get you in the district and then we'll have to cruise a bit until I find it. I'll know it when I see it. I've been there a couple of times but I forget the name of the place."

The cab driver was co-operative. He was also curious. If there were any spots in that district that he didn't know about he wanted to be sure he didn't remain too long in ignorance.

I sent him down one street, then back on another, suddenly said, "Here it is. That apartment house over there."

The cab driver pulled up and took a good look at the place. I paid him off and went in.

I guess Ernestine must have been sitting by the door with one hand on the knob. I'd no sooner given the first preliminary tap than the door opened wide. I went in.

"Oh, Donald!" she said. "I'm so thrilled! Donald, this is Bernice. You know all about her."

Bernice was a stunning-looking babe, a brunette with big, limpid eyes and curves that seemed to be trying to push their way through the clothes she was wearing. She certainly knew how to use those eyes and knew how to present her nylons to the best advantage.

"All right," I said to Ernestine, "what happened to-day?"

She said, "Bernie will help us, Donald."

I looked over at Bernice.

Bernice batted her eyes a couple of times and smiled, a tremulous, wistful smile.

It was easy to see that Bernice didn't need to eat at home except when she wanted to.

I said, "Are you still willing to help me, Ernestine?"

"Anything," she said, "Only . . ."

"Only what?" I asked.

"I have to co-operate with the police, too, you know."

"Why?"

"Well, they told me I did. They're working on a murder and—well, you know how it is."

"Sure," I said, "I understand."

I turned to Bernice. "How about you?" I said.

She made with the eyes and then smoothed down the hem of her skirt and ran the tips of her fingers nervously along her stocking. "What can I do?" she asked.

I said, "I want to know a few things about Evelyn Ellis that it may be the hotel wouldn't want you to talk about."

"I've told the police all I know."

"No, you haven't," I said, trying to follow the lead Ernestine had hinted at. "What about Evelyn's sex life?"

"I wouldn't know—except I guess there was plenty of it."

"Come on," I said, "this is for Ernestine. You're going to help her by telling me some of the things you know that I want to know."

"Well, she's considerably over twenty-one. I would say she wasn't entirely inexperienced—you wouldn't expect that, would you?"

"I wouldn't expect it," I said. "I'm not asking you if she's a virgin, if that's what you mean."

"I thought that's what you meant."

I said, "Bernice, quit stalling."

"What do you want to know?"

"About the Japanese photographer," I said.

"Oh, you mean the fellow with the rattling staccato voice —he's a dear."

"All right," I said. "What do you know about him?"

"Nothing. I've never met him. I know, of course, the number she calls, the Happy Daze Camera Company. They take model photographs and they've done all of her publicity photography."

"And there's a friendly relationship?"

"Oh, yes."

"How friendly?"

"I don't think she goes overboard with him, if that's what you mean, but ... it's a relationship that's hard to explain. He just worships the ground she walks on. She's his goddess, his inspiration. You know, I'll bet that he thinks she's a sweet, loyal, lovable girl and as pure as the driven snow."

"There have been quite a few telephone conversations?"

"She calls him quite frequently and I hear his voice on the line."

"What do they talk about?"

"I don't know. I didn't listen."

"Now," I said, "we're getting someplace. I'm going to have to put through a long-distance phone call. I'll get charges and give you the money to cover, but I want you, Bernice, to put through the call in your name. Then I'll talk."

"Whom do I call?" she asked.

"Carl Dover Christopher, the president of Christopher, Crowder and Doyle in Chicago. You'll have to get him at his home number. I don't think you'll have too much trouble. He's rather a wealthy man and a prominent man."

She laughed and said. "The number, in case you want it, is Madison 6-497183."

I tried to keep the surprise from registering. I said casually, "You've heard Inspector Hobart talking with him."

She said, "I don't know anything about that, but he's got a terrific crush on Evelyn. You know, she was a stenographer or something in one of the importing firms and the public relations man was looking for a model who could give a lot of cheesecake and get them some publicity. You know how it is. A newspaper photographer is naturally looking for something that will catch the eye. You can't get photographs of an exhibition of hardware and get any newspaper coverage. You have to——"

"Never mind that," I said. "Tell me about Carl Christopher."

"Well, I know that he met her back there and in some way he got her entered in the contest."

"How do you know?"

"Because when he came out here on a business trip about three weeks after the convention he telephoned Evelyn. She was in Los Angeles at the time and arranged to meet him there. She came up and stayed here at the hotel, registered under the name of Beverly Kettle. That's the first time I heard her other name of Evelyn Ellis. Mr. Christopher used to call for her as Evelyn Ellis. She asked us telephone girls to put through any calls that came for Evelyn Ellis to her room. She said Beverly Kettle was the name she was registered under but Evelyn Ellis was her stage name."

"Was she living with Carl Christopher for a while?" I asked.

"They had rooms on the same floor of the hotel. Nobody did any peeping at the keyhole. Mr. Christopher is an important man. He's the president of a big cutlery company, but . . . well, he was entertaining some customers and I guess he was being entertained himself and . . . anyway, I know they were friends and I know that Evelyn has called him—oh, a dozen times while she's been here in the hotel."

"At the company?" I asked, frowning. "Why didn't Inspector Hobart——"

"Oh, not at the company," she said. "She calls him at his club. That's his home number. He lives in a club. He's a widower and that's his private number at the club. Miss Ellis puts calls through station to station."

I went over to sit down on the davenport.

"You want me to call him?" Bernice asked.

I thought it over a minute and said, "I want you to call him very much indeed."

She went over to the phone, put through the call and within two minutes I heard a masculine voice with the tone of authority come booming over the line.

I said, "Mr. Christopher, this is an investigator working on that San Francisco homicide. I——"

"My God," he groaned. "Can't you folks give a man any peace at all? I've been talking with inspectors and detectives all day. I've told you all I know. I made it a point to look up the records personally so there'd be no——"

"That isn't what I wanted to talk to you about," I said.

"Well, what do you want to talk to me about?"

I said, "Have you made any special shipments of samples within the last few days because of any personal request that you might consider unusual?"

"No."

"Has anyone called you up and asked you to send out a rush sample of——"

"No."

I thought of Inspector Hobart and his condemnation of short cuts, his discounting brilliant detective work. I said, "All right, I'm sorry I had to bother you. I guess I was working on a bum lead."

He said, "Well, I wish you folks wouldn't disturb me. My God, I'm sorry I ever brought out the knife. And yet it's a good number."

"A ready sale?"

"Selling like hot cakes here in the East," he said.

"But no sales on the Coast?"

"No. We're getting a lot of repeat orders out of the East and our shipments have been limited. That's a very special grade of steel and you don't just turn that stuff out like the ordinary cutlery. That's real quality."

"You say your shipments are limited?" I asked.

"That's right," he said. "We don't do manufacturing on our numbers. We sell them. This is an imported article."

"Where's it from?" I asked.

"Japan. The blades are made in Sweden, the handles in Japan."

I gripped the receiver. "Where did you say?"

"Japan," he said. "What's the matter, haven't you got a good connection? I can hear *you* perfectly."

"Can you give me the name of the firm that does the manufacturing?"

"Not offhand," he said. "It's some kind of a jaw-breaking name."

I said, "How did you happen to get onto the article in

the first place? In other words, why should a knife made in Japan be brought to a cutlery company in Chicago and——"

"Because we can give them the best merchandising outlet they can possibly get," Christopher said. "The number was first called to our attention by a Japanese importing company here in Chicago."

"Oh, yes," I said. "I remember the background on that now. That was where Miss American Hardware worked, wasn't it?"

"I believe so. It was the Mizukaido Importing Company."

"Big importers?"

"That's right. They're big importers—represent a bunch of Japanese manufacturers, mostly heavy goods. They don't go in for the cameras, binoculars and other stuff, but cutlery mostly, and novelties and knick-knacks."

"Thanks," I told him. "I'm sorry. We'll try not to bother you again."

"Tell your men to try and get together on this stuff. What did you say your name was, Inspector?"

I gently slipped the phone back into the cradle.

"What is it, Donald?" Ernestine asked.

I said, "That's one of the pitfalls of investigative work. You get all loused up on sequences."

"What do you mean?" she asked.

I said, "Everybody looks up the distributor who sells those knives, Christopher, Crowder and Doyle. Nobody thinks of trying to find who supplies Christopher, Crowder and Doyle with their knives or when the first samples were brought into the country.

"Moreover, I'm so dumb it never occurred to me that a person doesn't get elected queen of the wholesale hardware convention and become Miss American Hardware and then have portraits taken in a bathing suit. The portraits come first."

"Of course they come first," Bernice said. "I tried out for one of those jobs once. This was a credit association meeting. All applicants had to be photographed and accompany their applications with bathing-suit photographs."

"Did you win?" I asked.

"No."

"How come?"

"I was dumb. I thought the bathing suit I was to be photographed in should be the bathing suit I was going to wear for the final judging. Some of the other girls were more generous."

"You mean Bikini bathing suits?"

"I mean Bikini bathing suits," she said. "They attracted the attention of the nominating committee—in a big way."

I said to her, "Listen, Bernice, I've got to get in that hotel. I want to get in so that no one knows I'm in the hotel. You've been there for a while. You know the bell captain who's on nights. I want to talk with him on the phone."

"But why can't you just walk right in and——"

"He's hot," Ernestine said. "Don't you understand, Bernie? He's hotter than a stove lid. If he's going to case the joint he's got to do it under cover."

I looked at her and tried to keep from smiling at the way she'd picked up crook lingo from the television. All it needed was one look at her eager countenance and her sparkling eyes to see how she was so engrossed in this thing that she had completely lost sight of all of her inhibitions.

Bernice said, "This bell captain is ... I've been out with him a couple of times."

"That's fine," I told her, "he'll do what you want."

"I don't know. I didn't do what he wanted."

"Then he'll be sure to," I said. 'Get him on the phone. Tell him it's a favor."

"What do you want?"

"I want to talk with him."

Bernice dialed the hotel and asked for the bell captain by name. After a moment she nodded, "His name is Chris," she said.

I said, "Hello, Chris. I have a favor I want you to do for me."

"Who is this talking?"

"I'm a friend of Bernice."

"Yeah?" he asked, and his voice was suddenly cold.

"I haven't seen her in years," I said. "I'm from Los Angeles. I looked her up because I wanted to get your name."

"Oh, yeah?" he said, and this time there was a note of curiosity in his voice but the cold enmity was gone.

I said, "I want to get in the hotel. I have fifty bucks that says you're going to help me."

"Fifty bucks is awfully damned eloquent," he said. "What do you want?"

I said, "I want you to come up to Bernice's apartment and bring a bell boy's uniform. I'm going to put it on and go back to the hotel with you."

There was silence for a moment. Then he said, "I might get into trouble over this."

"Not if no one knew anything about it," I said.

"Well, people have a way of finding those things out and——"

"Okay," I said. "It's a business proposition with me. I'm a magazine writer working on a story in connection with the murder. I can peddle the story for five hundred bucks. I'm willing to pay something for expenses but I'm not going to give *you* all of *my* profits and then turn around and give some more to the Government. If you don't want to do it, forget it."

"I want to do it," he said hastily.

"All right," I said. "Bring the uniform up to Bernice's apartment. Can you get a uniform?"

"That's no trouble," he said, "but I don't know your size. I——"

I said, "Bernice can tell you about the size."

I turned to Bernice and said, "Bernice, you know the boys there at the hotel. Is there one of them who's about my size and build?"

Bernice looked me over for a moment, then said, "Tell him to get a suit that would fit Eddie."

I said, "Bernice said get a suit that would——"

"I heard her," he said. "She's there, huh? How long have *you* been there?"

"Just got in."

"Okay," he said, "I'm coming right up."

Bernice seemed thoughtful and a little worried but Ernestine was so excited she could hardly sit down. She'd stay put for a minute or two, then get up and run out of the kitchen to get a drink of water.

I had a chance to do some thinking before Chris got there.

I could see why Bernice hesitated after I saw Chris. He looked Bernice over the way a cattle buyer would inspect a steer that he was thinking about putting in a feed lot. With him, Bernice was merchandise.

The uniform fitted me as though it had been tailored for me.

I gave Chris fifty bucks. He had his own car outside.

"I want to borrow a couple of suitcase," I told Ernestine. She dug out the suitcases: one of hers, one of Bernice's.

"Will we get these back?" Bernice asked suspiciously.

"Of course you will, Bernie," Ernestine said before I could say a word. "Mr. Lam is——"

I gave her a warning look.

"A reputable magazine writer," she finished. "You've read his stuff in lots of the magazines. Your suitcase is just as safe with him as it would be right there in the closet."

I loaded the suitcases with some extra newspapers and magazines to give them weight. On the way back to the hotel I said to Chris, "Now, I'll want a passkey and——"

"Whoa, back up," he said. "We don't give passkeys to *anyone*."

"I thought the passkey was included in the seventy-dollar——"

"*Seventy*. You gave me fifty."

"The hell I did! It wasn't seventy?"

"It was fifty."

"Well, it should have been seventy," I said, "and that, of course, included the passkey."

"Say," he said, "you're a fast worker."

I said, "When I go in with the suitcases you just walk around, pick up the passkey and hand it to me."

"It's fastened to the big metal ring," he said. "It——"

"I don't care what it's fastened to," I told him. "I want the passkey."

"That could cost me my job."

"Well," I said, "perhaps I was right, after all. It only was a fifty-dollar job."

"All right, give me the additional twenty," he said.

I gave him the twenty.

We got to the hotel and I barged in, carrying the suit-cases, with my head down and my shoulders forward as though the suitcases were plenty heavy.

Chris walked around behind the clerk's desk, said some-thing to the clerk, received a nod in return, and came back carrying a passkey which was chained to a wide metal loop.

He handed me the passkey and turned away.

I went to the elevators, up to the seventh floor, got off the elevator and started knocking on doors.

The first door I tried brought a big man in shirtsleeves in his stocking feet, to the door.

"You phone the bell captain to send these suitcases up here?" I asked.

He said, "No," and closed the door, hard.

I tried two more rooms and got turned down on both occasions.

There was no answer at the third room. I made sure no one was going to answer, then I fitted the passkey and opened the door.

The bed was made up, the towels were all neat, there was no baggage in the room. It was an unoccupied room.

I parked the suitcases and the passkey, made certain that the catch on the door was fixed so it would remain un-locked, went out into the corridor and walked down to Evelyn Ellis' room.

I listened for a moment to make certain that she didn't have company. I couldn't hear any voices.

I tapped on the door.

Evelyn opened the door.

She was all dolled up in filmy stuff that made a sort of aura around a naked body as she stood in the doorway with the bright light behind her. I could see she'd fixed herself up in her most seductive garb, and she'd put in a lot of time being certain that it was sufficiently revealing. With the light behind her it was quite a sight. She evidently was expecting someone she wanted to impress.

"You!" she said, and started to slam the door.

I lowered a shoulder, charged the door, shot it out of her hand, and walked in.

She looked at me with concentrated venom. "So now

you're a bell boy! Well, Mr. Lam, you're getting out, and getting out now," she said. "If you don't I'll call——"

"The police again?" I asked. "*That* would be interesting."

"Damn you!" she said.

I said, "Sit down, Evelyn. You may as well take it easy. The Chinese have a saying, you know, about things that are inevitable and about relaxation."

"You'd be surprised how many times I've heard that," she said.

I walked over to a chair and sat down. I said, "Let's try putting things together. Who's your friend in the Mizukaido Importing Company?"

She said, "I could spit on you! You are the most contemptible, snooping——"

I said, "Don't go flying off the handle before you know what I'm here for. I'm trying to help you out and tearing off your clothes won't work this time. Whether you know it or not, you're on a spot."

"What do you mean, on the spot?"

I said, "My wife and I rented the apartment in Los Angeles after you moved out. I put my trunk in the garage. I can prove that you deliberately switched trunks so that you could trap Standley Downer into picking up my trunk instead of his. Then you had his trunk sent to you. You found a secret compartment in it, got fifty grand out of it, and then had no further use for Standley Downer.

"You were working with the Mizukaido Importing Company in Chicago. You met Carl Christopher. He was a big shot in the hardware industry. He took an interest in you. You started selling him things. Then Jasper Diggs Calhoun, the public relations man, got the idea of a Miss American Hardware to show cheesecake and pulchritudinous curves for a publicity background to advertise the convention.

"I imagine Mr. Christopher was either on the nominating committee or else he was the one who did the selecting.

"He selected you. It was through his influence you got the job and got the publicity. You have taken various occasions and various methods of expressing gratitude."

"All right," she said. "So what? I had the winning figure, didn't I?"

"How would I know?" I asked.

She looked me over carefully, speculatively, thoughtfully. "Want to take a look?" she asked challengingly. She stood up and started fumbling with a fastener some place. Then she paused seductively. "Well, Donald?"

"Are you trying to change the subject?" I asked.

"Are you?" she wanted to know.

It was at that moment the door, which had not been fully closed, pushed open and Bertha Cool, attired in a gray business suit, came striding into the room.

"Never mind, dearie," she said. "Keep your clothes on. You're not dealing with a man now. You're going to talk to me."

"Who are you, and what are you doing in here?" Evelyn demanded. "How dare you come striding in here in this way? How dare you?——"

Bertha reached out, put a hand on Evelyn's chest and gave a push. Evelyn came down on the davenport so hard I saw her head jar.

"Don't pull that line with me," Bertha said. "I don't let trollops get upstage with me."

Bertha turned to me. "I was outside the door long enough to hear your summary of the situation. Now what the hell are you after?"

"Right now," I said, "I'm trying to find the murderer of Standley Downer. I *was* in a position to make some pretty good progress when you came barging in and upset the apple cart."

"Phooey!" Bertha said. "I got here just in time. When a babe like this starts talking about what she used to win the bathing beauty contest, you're in the first stages of a trance.

"Tell me what you want out of this bitch and *I'll* get it."

I said, "She worked for the Mizukaido Importing Company. She became friendly with Carl Christopher of the firm of Christopher, Crowder and Doyle, who are big cutlery distributors, among other things.

"Evelyn started going out with Carl. When a very interesting development in steel carving knives came along,

Evelyn told the importing company she thought she could interest Christopher, Crowder and Doyle.

"She did.

"When it came time to select a Miss American Hardware for the New Orleans convention, with a lot of newspaper publicity, some Hollywood screen tests, some television appearances and all that goes with it, Evelyn decided she'd been working long enough. She put the bug on her friend, Carl Christopher. He told her to have some bathing beauty shots made and sent in to the nominating committee. He also told her she'd better have them made on the Coast and better have a Coast address so it wouldn't appear that he was pulling for one of his friends.

"As nearly as I can put two and two together, Evelyn went to her grateful Japanese friends in the importing company and they put her in touch with Takahashi Kisarazu at the Happy Daze Camera Company.

"Now then, I was just going to take it from there when you burst in and——"

"And a damn good thing I did," Bertha said. "She was getting ready to give you the full treatment. Give a babe like that an hour alone with an impressionable little bastard like you and you wouldn't be worth a damn.

"Now I'll take over and——"

The phone rang.

Before Bertha could reach it, Evelyn had picked it up, said, "Hello ... I have company at the moment——" Her voice showed sudden enthusiasm. "Why, yes, Inspector Hobart," she said. "I'll be only *too* glad to see you. There are some people here, but I think they're just leaving. Why don't you come on up? There *is* someone with you? Well, that's wonderful.... No, no, not at all. I'll be glad to see you. Come on up."

She stood there at the phone, smiling. I figured Bertha could take care of herself. I knew I was going to have my hands full taking care of myself. I shot out the door, dashed down the corridor, went into the vacant room where I'd planted the suitcases, locked the door, and waited.

It was a job just sitting there and waiting. I could hear my heart pounding. I heard the elevator doors clang. I heard steps in the corridor.

I waited for a while for things to quiet down, then I took the two suitcases, ran to the door marked STAIRS, dashed down three flights of stairs, then rang for the elevator and came down in my bell boy uniform, carrying the two suitcases out through the lobby to the front.

The clerk slammed his palm down on a bell and yelled, "Front!" Then yelled "Boy! Oh, boy! ... hey, *you*!"

I put the two suitcases down.

"Take Mr. Jackson to 813," he said. "Unless you———"

I looked at the man who had given the name of Jackson. It was none other than my friend, Jasper Diggs Calhoun, of Los Angeles. He didn't recognize me in the bell boy uniform, standing there with the suitcases.

I said, "I'm taking them out to a guest who's waiting for a cab in the front," I said.

"Oh, all right," the clerk said. He turned to Calhoun and said, "Just a moment, Mr. Jackson. I'll have another boy here."

The clerk slammed his palm down on the bell. "Front!" he called.

I picked up the two suitcases, then went out to the sidewalk. Fortunately there was a cab there. I handed the suitcases to the cab driver. He stowed the suitcases, then stood there waiting expectantly for a guest to come out.

I jumped in the cab and said, "I'm delivering the suitcases to an apartment straight down the street."

We got away from there, down the street and around the corner. There were no red lights, no siren, no whistles, nothing.

I heaved a sigh of relief.

I told the cabbie to wait in front of the apartment house. I delivered the suitcases to the apartment and told Bernice and Ernestine that it might be just as well if they failed to remember anything that had happened. I changed my clothes in the bathroom, gave Bernice the uniform I'd worn, went back to the cab and had the driver take me out to within about five blocks of the Ocean Beach Hotel.

I walked down through the alley, reconnoitered the fire escape, grabbed the end of the cord, pulled the section of iron stairway down to its lowest position, jumped up, caught the iron rail and hoisted myself up to the stairs. I untied the light rope, wrapped it around my body and climbed the fire escape.

I got to the floor I wanted, slipped in through the window and went down to the room Hazel had rented.

I started to put the key in the lock and then heard the phone ringing, steadily, insistently.

That was something I hadn't counted on. If I answered and police heard a man's voice they'd know what had happened. If no one answered they'd wonder where the hell Hazel was and probably would put two and two together.

I dashed down the corridor, tapped gently on the door of my room.

Hazel, attired only in panties and bra, opened it, started to say something, then caught herself. I dragged her out in the corridor, handed her the key to her room. "Get down there fast," I whispered. "The phone is ringing. They're checking up on you. Tell them you were in the bathroom."

"I'm half naked," she whispered. "I slipped my dress off——"

"Get started," I said, and gave her a slap on the behind as I opened the door to my room, tiptoed inside, coughed a couple of times, then yawned sleepily.

I went to the bathroom, washed the dirt of the fire escape off my hands, and was just returning when the door surreptitiously opened and Hazel came in.

I frowned at her.

She gestured toward the scanties she was wearing by way of explanation, walked over to the closet, took a dress from the hanger and stood looking at me, hesitating somewhat. Her eyes were sultry and inviting.

Abruptly the telephone shattered the silence of the room.

I let it ring five or six times, then went over and picked up the receiver and said sleepily, "Hello."

Inspector Hobart's voice said, "Hello, Lam. I guess I woke you up."

"I suppose," I said angrily, "you want some more ideas."

"I thought you'd like to know," Inspector Hobart said, "that down in Los Angeles, Dover C. Inman, proprietor of the Full Dinner Pail, has just made a confession to Sergeant Frank Sellers, admitting that he and Herbert Baxley were in partnership on that armored car deal.

"The two drivers of the car had got sweet on a couple of the babes who were car hopping and Inman put it up to them to get the keys out of the pockets of the driver and the guard. I don't need to tell you how they did it, but Inman got the waxed impressions of the keys, had duplicate keys made, and when the armored car stopped for coffee, Baxley pretended to be changing a tire. He had his car parked right in back of the armored truck. He knew that there was a shipment of one hundred thousand dollars in thousand-dollar bills being sent to one of the banks on the order of Standley Downer. Downer wanted to get his money in the form of cash because he was planning on going bye-bye with Evelyn Ellis. Baxley had a tip from a friend of Evelyn's.

"Under the circumstances, Frank Sellers is feeling pretty damn good. He's even friendly toward you. He recovered all but six thousand dollars of the money. He's vindicated his own name, solved the armored car case, and told me to tell you he always had been a friend of yours—that you exasperated him at times by your cocksure manner, but he thought you were, to use his own words, 'one swell little bastard.'

"So," Inspector Hobart said, "you're out of quarantine, Lam. You can do anything you damn please. Incidentally, as you probably know, your little girl friend, Hazel, is registered in your hotel under the name of Hazel Bickley. She's in Room 417, which is on your same floor. You might like to give her a ring."

"She's here?"

"That's right."

"You put her in here at this hotel?"

"She put herself there," Inspector Hobart said. "I was baiting a trap. You were the bait. Her attorney kept ringing up and pestering for your release so we gave him a definite time. That was so he could have his client alerted and she could follow you. The officer who drove you out to the hotel certainly had to act dumb to keep from '*discovering*' her tagging along. My God, the opinion you amateurs must have of cops!"

"Wait a minute," I said. "If Frank Sellers recovered the

loot from that armored car job, what the hell happened to the fifty grand I got?"

"That's your hard luck, Lam," he said. "Sergeant Sellers had a theft from an armored truck. He solved that. I've got a murder case. I haven't solved that—not yet.

"You've lost fifty grand. You haven't solved that, and my guess is, you're not going to.

"We've all got our troubles. All God's chillun got troubles."

"Hey, wait a minute," I said. "Have you seen Evelyn Ellis within the last couple of hours?"

"Nope. We shook her room down, didn't find anything, and she's off the list—at least for the present. Now, in case you're planning on any nocturnal confidential conferences—and you'll notice I'm being very tactful—with your client, Hazel Clune, alias Hazel Downer, alias Hazel Bickley, I might warn you that the room you're in is bugged. We've been having you under audible surveillance ever since you went in there. We even have a tape recording of your talk with Hazel."

"The hell!" I said.

Inspector Hobart chuckled. "I can't say I admire your taste in television programs, Lam. You were doing so much master-minding that I thought sure you'd tune in on these Hollywood private-eye programs. I hardly expected you to suffer through all the romantic agonies of a sickening love story on television, but damned if you didn't stay with it. I——"

"Hey, wait a minute," I said. "You weren't in the Caltonia Hotel? You didn't go up to see Evelyn Ellis tonight?"

"No, not within the last two hours."

I said, "Look, Inspector, do me a favor. It'll take me about thirty-five minutes to get up to that hotel. Will you go up there with me?"

"Why?"

"I've got something hot."

"Another one of your brilliant ideas?"

"That's right."

"Well, for your information," he said, "I'm going home and then going to bed. I'm not going to go running around the city at night just because you have some brilliant ideas you want to tell me about."

I said, "Inspector, this is important. Please——"

"Forget it," he snapped. "You've had enough brain storms for one day."

I said, "All right. Let me tell you something. Evelyn worked for the Mizukaido Importing Company. This was before she ever became Miss American Hardware. Carl Christopher, president of the Christopher, Crowder and Doyle Cutlery Company, fell for her. She used the contact to feather her own nest and also to sell a big order for the Mizukaido Importing Company, for which she probably got a commission. The big order, in case you're interested, was the exclusive United States distributorship of the thin carving sets made of imported Swedish steel and with a synthetic plastic handle made to resemble onyx.

"Outside of the manager of the Japanese importing company she was the first person in the United States to have one of those carving knives. She took a sample up and sold Carl Christopher on them. Now then, do you want to——"

"Hell's bells!" he said, and slammed up the telephone.

I turned to Hazel who was standing there sweetly seductive, holding the dress in one hand.

"Get it on, kid, get it on!" I yelled at her. "We're fighting minutes. The sonofabitch is going to short cut me and go up to Evelyn's room."

I jiggled the phone until the desk answered and said, "Get me a taxi and get it quick."

CHAPTER ELEVEN

I BRIBED the cab driver to hit the high spots. We pulled up in front of the hotel within twenty-two minutes of the time Inspector Hobart had hung up the telephone.

"Come on, Hazel," I said, and holding her hand, we streaked through the door of the hotel over to the elevators and up to the seventh floor.

I hurried Hazel down to Evelyn Ellis' room and tried the door.

It was unlocked.

I have never seen such a wreckage as was in that room. Evelyn Ellis had a heavy flannel bathrobe wrapped around her, and was crying. The torn remnants of the fluffy negligee were scattered around the apartment. Evelyn had a right eye that was slowly swelling shut and she was frightened.

Big Bertha Cool stood in the middle of the floor, her arms akimbo, looking at the wreckage.

Inspector Hobart had been taking notes. He looked just a little dazed.

He looked up when I came in and didn't seem the least surprised. He looked like a man who couldn't be surprised by anything any more.

Bertha looked at me and said, "What the hell did *you* run out for? For God's sake, don't you know that old telephone gag? Some guy calls up and she says, 'Why, yes, Inspector, come on up here.' God Almighty, you went tearing out of here. . . . That was just some buddy of hers wanting to come up here. He just called to find out if the coast was clear. The minute she said she had people with her the guy hung up in a panic. From where I was, I was able to hear the click on the line. She went on talking after he hung up and pulled all that Inspector Hobart stuff out of thin air just in order to scare you."

I looked at Bertha and said, "What *are* you talking about? You have me mixed up with someone else. You remember our client, Bertha. This is Hazel."

Hobart stared at Bertha, said, "You're all wet, Mrs.

161

Cool. Lam hasn't been out of his room all night. We've had him under auditory surveillance. Don't try to hand me a line!"

Bertha started to say something, but changed her mind.

I faced Bertha and said, "What's the score?"

"This little bitch," Bertha said, "was carrying on with a publicity director by the name of Calhoun. She liked him but he didn't have dough. When Standley Downer cut in with dough, our little friend Evelyn here took a powder on Calhoun.

"Calhoun was jealous. He didn't like it. He managed to locate Downer, came up here and found Downer and little Evelyn together just at a time when Downer was unpacking your trunk and found he had the wrong trunk.

"He tried to explain to Evelyn that this was a big surprise to him, that he had a lot of dough and someone had highjacked it by switching trunks. That was a line Evelyn thought she had heard before. She said things that weren't ladylike.

"Then Calhoun busted in just as Evelyn had said dirty words to Standley and Standley was proceeding to choke the hell out of her.

"Calhoun picked up a carving knife out of a set that was on the dresser and stuck it into Downer's back."

"Will you kindly tell me," Inspector Hobart said, "where in hell that carving knife actually came from? Excuse me, I didn't mean to say hell in front of women."

Bertha looked at him with glittering eyes and said, "Why the hell not? I always figure that a woman who faints every time she hears some sonofabitch swear is just putting on an act anyway. Now, what was it you wanted to know? The carving knife—oh, yes, the nice homely little touch to the thing. This all took place in a housekeeping suite with a kitchen. Little Evelyn and Standley were going to be all cozy and not go out for a while. They were going to have a nice little honeymoon. So Evelyn made a contribution to the furnishings. She kicked in with a carving set.

"After Calhoun used the knife Evelyn got him out of there. She had him take the fancy box with the fork and steel with him. She said she'd take care of the murder weapon. She told him to take a plane back home. She promised to join him later. I guess he's there now waiting for this bitch to make good.

"After she got rid of Calhoun," Bertha said, "little Miss Smartie Pants here opened up the clothing on the corpse and found a money belt with seventy-five one-thousand-dollar bills in it. So she naturally appropriated the money.

"Then she looked through the clothes in the trunk and found a note that the trunk apparently belonged to a guy named George Biggs Gridley who was staying at the Golden Gateway Hotel. She didn't make the mistake of leaving any messages for Gridley nor did she try calling from her room, but she used up four dollars' worth of dimes calling the Golden Gateway Hotel from the phone booth in the lobby and asking to be connected with Mr. Gridley.

"The knife and chamois-skin belt she put in a brief case she had here in the room, took it downstairs, casually dropped it among the incoming baggage and went on about her business.

"She did all her cover-up stuff before the body was discovered. Standley Downer was a big-shot gambler who was going to take a powder. He was getting all of his stuff in thousand-dollar bills. But he was afraid of being high-graded, so he wouldn't put all of his eggs in one basket. He carried seventy-five grand in the money belt, had fifty thousand stashed in his trunk. The fact that the armored car lost the bank's money was no skin off Standley's nose. The shipment was insured. The bank paid Standley and kept quiet about it."

Evelyn simply sat there, completely wilted, sobbing.

Hazel, her eyes as big as saucers stood listening.

Hobart said, "Well, we'll pick Calhoun up in Los Angeles. We——"

I said, "Just a minute, please." I stepped over to the phone, picked it up and said to the clerk, "Will you tell Mr. Jackson in Room 813 that a police officer is in the hotel and had asked him to step down to the room of Evelyn Ellis in Room 751?"

I hung up the phone and said to Inspector Hobart, "Come on, we've just got time."

He hesitated a second or two, then followed me out into the hall.

We dashed for the stairs and up to 813.

We had just about reached the door when it burst open and Calhoun, dragging a suitcase, came tearing out, an expression of wild-eyed panic on his face.

"Hello, Calhoun," I said. "Remember me? I'm Lam. Shake hands with Inspector Hobart."

Hobart took one look at Calhoun, then reached back to his belt to pull out the handcuffs. When he had them adjusted, he turned and looked at me.

"Now, how the hell did you know the guy was here in this hotel registered under the name of Jackson?" he asked.

"Inspector," I said, "you've just got to put it down to some of that brilliant reasoning that comes from watching television programs. Anyone who had followed the private-eye programs would know he *had* to be here in the hotel in order to enable us to get the crime solved in thirty minutes, including commercials."

Inspector Hobart drew back his hand to hit me. He was white he was so mad. Then he took a deep breath and said, "I'm grateful to you, Lam. Also, I'm beginning to know exactly how Frank Sellers feels."

We marched Calhoun down to the room where Evelyn Ellis was being guarded by Bertha Cool.

Calhoun took one look at the militant Bertha Cool, at the sobbing Evelyn, and knew the jig was up. He started blabbing out the story.

He knew Evelyn had given him the double-cross. He knew that Downer was planning to go to San Francisco and fix up a place and he and Evelyn were going to start housekeeping. So Calhoun made it a point to ring up her apartment, pretending to be a gangster, with his voice disguised, and leave grim warnings for Downer that he had just so many hours to pay up or else.

"In other words," I said to Calhoun, "there was, right then, in the back of your mind, the idea that you might kill Downer in order to get him out of the way."

"No, no, no, no!" he yammered hysterically. "I swear it! I swear it!"

"Baloney," Hobart said. "I don't know whether we can prove it on you or not, but I think we can—self-defense, hell, this is premeditation. It's first degree."

164

"He was defending me," Evelyn sobbed.

"That's *your* story," Hobart said. "We'll see how it stands up." He turned to me and said, "Okay, this is where you two came in. You get the hell out of here, and I mean out of town, and if you so much as open your yap to a newspaper reporter until you get out of here I'll see that you never set foot in San Francisco again without having the whole damn police force trail you around.

"I'm going to give you a police escort down to the airport. You're going down there so fast you'll establish a record, just as fast as sirens and a red light can get you there.

"Then I'm going to take this precious pair down to Headquarters and we're going to wrap this thing up by good old police methods.

"And when you get to Los Angeles don't give out any stories to the newspaper reporters. Frank Sellers has already told about how he recovered the dough down there and I'll be telling him about how I solved the murder case up here. You can put in your time, Lam, trying to figure what happened to that fifty grand, provided you ever had it."

"I don't need to put in my time on it," I said. "I know where it is now."

"Where?"

I said, "I was a damn fool not to think of it before."

"All right," he said, "you've got me sold. Where is it?"

I pointed my finger at Bertha Cool. "All right, Bertha, kick through," I said.

Bertha's face purpled with anger for a minute, then she said, "You had me so goddamned scared I almost fainted. I opened that damn camera box so I could see what was in it and send it back, and I opened that box of photographic paper and out tumbled thousand-dollar bills all over the place. I scooped up the money, put it in my desk, and then the phone rang and Frank Sellers was telling me about you and I knew damned well you'd left me sitting in the middle with a lot of hot money. So I dashed down to the photographic store, bought another box of enlarging paper just like the one you'd had, cut the seals with my penknife, stuck it back in the box, took the carton out to the reception room and told Dorris Fisher to wrap it up and send it back to the damn camera company for credit.

"Fifty grand of hot money! My God, I haven't slept——"

I turned to Hazel and grinned. "It wasn't hot," I said to Bertha, "just pleasantly warm."

"*My* money?" Hazel asked.

"Sure it's your money," I said.

"You're going to have a hell of a time proving it, dearie," Bertha told her.

"No, she isn't," I said. "I have a letter signed by Standley Downer in which he admits he had given it to her. Downer was a big-time bookie. He had one weakness—he liked the babes. After Evelyn came along he decided he's trade Hazel in on a new model."

"One that had even *more* mileage," Hazel said cattily.

Evelyn didn't even raise her head. She was licked. Hazel gave a little squeal and melted in my arms, her hot, grateful lips clinging to mine. "Donald," she whispered, "these bills you found, did they have the corners cut off?"

"If they didn't when I found them," I whispered, "they will have by the time Bertha produces them. She isn't going to let a fat fee slip through *her* diamond-studded fingers.... Frankly, Hazel, I was working too fast to notice. However, I think that——"

Bertha said, "For God's sake, cut out this damn lolly-gagging."

Inspector Hobart said into the phone, "Get me a squad car up here with a red light and a siren and the best damn driver you've got. I want to get two people down to the airport so fast the dust doesn't have a chance to settle."

He slammed up the phone and turned to me and shook his head. "You goddammed amateurs!" he said.

>>> If you've enjoyed this book and would like to discover more great vintage crime and thriller titles, as well as the most exciting crime and thriller authors writing today, visit: >>>

The Murder Room
Where Criminal Minds Meet

themurderroom.com

www.ingramcontent.com/pod-product-compliance
Ingram Content Group UK Ltd.
Pitfield, Milton Keynes, MK11 3LW, UK
UKHW022309280225
455674UK00004B/228